from the
outside

Praise for *From the Outside*

"A real page turner. Ms Harrison combines gripping excitement with a sympathetic treatment of her characters which makes the reader really care about them."
                                                    —DIANE KRATZ

"A privilege to explore and understand the inter-generational trauma passed down through three generations, portrayed in a personal memoir. A triumph of personal and familial survival."—KRISTIN CONSTANCE

"Resonant and brave. Once I started reading, I couldn't put this book down."
                                                    —LINDA KILBY

"The way Heidi Harrison weaves her own story of growing up, and of her mother's harrowing journey during the war years and afterward provides a framework to help identify and understand the concept of generational trauma."
                                                    —PETER JENNY

"A deeply moving and compelling story where the author's bravery through her journey of self-discovery honours her Jewish heritage and those who were part of her remarkable lineage. A tale where, incidentally, a generational suppressed grief and harrowing fear shapes the blossoming of courage and enormous desire for deep healing."
                                                    —JEY IBARRA

"Riveting, traumatic Holocaust escape journeys across continents."

— Sue Shimer

"This hauntingly beautiful book chronicles a Jewish family's perilous escape from Nazi-occupied Poland, their survival in Stalin's Gulag, and their eventual journey to freedom. The author skillfully weaves this epic tale with the granddaughter's poignant reflections on how inherited trauma shaped her emotional world. A lyrical exploration of survival, memory, and the enduring impact of unspoken pain across generations."

—Jesse Stimson

"Beautifully written. I couldn't put it down. Powerful and raw and so deeply moving."

—Manjari Newman

From the Outside is an autobiographical insight of Heidi's journey as a second generational child. The seeds of her family's extraordinary escapes and travels during the second world war are explained and contained. They grow in her and are pruned. The intergenerational trauma occurs with historical events, as well as the personal suffering and hopes of the family. History of survival and loss is often quietly inferred in families, but here is it spoken out loud."

—Margaret Kaye

Other books by Heidi Harrison

The Four Seasons

When Paris Was Her Lover

Quand Paris Était Son Amour

from the outside

Heidi Harrison

EMERALD HOUSE PUBLISHING
www.emeraldhpublishing.com

Printed in the United States of America
First Edition – October 2024

Cover Design by Sharon Blyth-Moss
Book Design by Gorham Printing

To my mom, always.

Chapter One

From the outside, it was an ordinary fence, wooden beams, around five and a half feet high, maybe less. It served its purpose: to keep everything out. No one paid much attention to the house that was behind it. Any number of secrets could have been going on, and not a soul would have known. I imagined that is what the owners wanted. Every morning, I would walk down the street, past that fence. I walked right past it and for so many years I never even paused to wonder if there was even a house on the other side.

One day, though, years later, I don't know what made me stop to stand on my tiptoes and peer over the edge. What I saw shocked me enormously. There were things on the other side of the fence that astounded me. It was hideous, yet intriguing. I yearned to know more. I was immediately pulled into a story that had nothing to do with me, but at the same time had everything to do with me.

After that day, after having perused the contours of the space behind the fence, I realized that for much of my life, I had been like a sheep: following what I was supposed to follow, seeing what I was prescribed to see, conducting my life from the obvious.

Without even knowing it, I had developed a lack of originality, a hesitancy towards and even an abhorrence of curiosity. Perhaps all the people around me were just like me, as I never saw anyone peer over the edge of that fence. That's why the fence worked so well. None of us ever had the gumption to see the one thing that those who had it built did not want us to notice.

But I did not look over the top of that fence until later in life. Much later.

* * *

I went to a therapist once when I was about fourteen. Why did I go? Because my mother told me to. I was a good kid. I did what my mother told me to do, even when I was a teenager.

"I think you need to see a therapist, Helen," my mother asserted one day as I was setting the table for dinner, my daily chore. I had been particularly quiet that week, as I recall. Maybe I hadn't talked to my mom at all. I don't really remember.

"Why?"

"I think you are depressed."

"What makes you think that?"

My mother looked up. Her face looked worried. I think she was rather astonished that I said something. I was surprised too that she surmised I was depressed. I didn't think my mom paid attention to things that weren't obvious. I didn't think anyone, including myself, had any idea about feelings. Was I depressed? True, sometimes I imagined killing myself, or just not being on this planet, but that was my secret, I thought. I used to pride myself on my vagueness towards the outside world.

"I have booked an appointment for you with someone I think you'll like. And if you don't, at least talk to her. I think she can help you."

That was just like my mom. Trying to help, but not quite sure how. When one is disconnected from one's own feelings, it is nearly impossible to really understand others. For example, when I was ten, she volunteered to talk to my girl scout troop about sex. I think she felt that all girls should know something about how babies are born. I think the underlying agenda for her was to instruct us about birth control, but that was never spoken of. She did not even mention the word "sex" that afternoon. I walked away from that "talk" wondering if babies get born when you poop in the toilet. For weeks I forced myself to be constipated and refused to eat vegetables, which, I had read, made you poop more.

The therapist looked at me, and she shook her head. I refused to talk to her. I refused to talk to anyone. I had dreams of being famous, of being someone, and of being noticed, but all of that was just a dream. What was real was that I had so many thick walls that kept me inside. Besides, it was my prescription to not notice anything, to be numb to a world that seemed so very far away. It felt like my destiny to be concealed behind those walls.

Before I left the session that day, the therapist suggested that I talk to someone, if not with her, about how my mother's trauma has affected me.

"What trauma?" I asked. I think I was rather belligerent. "There is no trauma!"

"Your mother told me a bit of her past."

"I have no idea what you are talking about." I think I was screaming. If not, then I am sure my voice was raised to a higher decibel than I was accustomed to.

I don't know how, but she was quite calm after my outburst, and she looked me straight in the eye. I wanted to throw her to the ground. Instead, I slammed the door and ran down the stairs of that building. I had never experienced such a display of emotion in me. I was shocked.

Chapter Two

On the 23rd of August 1939 the German and Russian governments signed the Ribbentrop-Molotov Pact. Some people called it the Hitler-Stalin Pact or the Nazi-Soviet Pact. It was a secret treaty of non-aggression that divided Eastern and Central Europe between them.

On the 1st of September 1939 Germany invaded Poland. Sixteen days later, on the 17th of September, the Red Army entered Poland.

Between February and March of 1940, the Red Army forcibly expelled 1.5 million Polish civilians (as well as Ukrainians and Belorussians) from their homes in the eastern side of Poland, the land that the Russians deemed theirs. They shoved them into filthy cattle cars and took them to labor camps in Siberia and Kazakhstan. There were four mass deportations that occurred.

The Red Army called it ethnic cleansing.

* * *

My mother, Ewa, was born in 1930 in Cracow, Poland. Her life was simple and happy in the sense that she had no worries, and her parents made sure that their children's existence was protected. Her mother, Gosia, was more interested in her political endeavors and her intellectual prowess, however, than in mothering. Her father, Andrzej, while doting on his eldest daughter, was a tyrant, and he had high expectations for his children. Agata, the maid, took care of the essential upbringing of Ewa and her sister Agnieszka, who was born seven years later. She allowed the children to feel cared for and have innocent childhoods.

But the one thing that neither a parent nor a nanny could ever do was to control the world around them.

* * *

In 1938, the persecution of Jews in Europe became virulent. Her last summer vacation, in 1939, at a picturesque resort on the Vistula River near Kazimierz, was filled with splashing in the fresh water and collecting seashells in the soft sand. Everyone wanted to prolong their carefree lives. Her parents knew though, that the world was changing. (At the end of August, they returned to their home in Radom, where they had recently moved because the company where Andrzej was working was transferred. He was the chief engineer of a factory that manufactured military equipment. Radom was further inland and east, and strategically it was supposed to be safe.)

World War Two broke out on the first of September 1939. My mother was nine years old.

On the third of September German bombs started falling on Radom, and every few minutes my mother's family had to look for shelter. My mother put her hands over her ears. The sounds were so loud, there was so much smoke. At one point she went outside and saw a dead person lying just outside their door.

"Mommy is he dead?" she asked. Gosia didn't answer. Andrzej didn't answer. Even Agata didn't answer. They were all busy arguing about where to go to be safe from the bombs. Her sister was asleep in Agata's arms.

"Shhh…" her father said. No talking."

Ewa kept her mouth shut as the adults told her what to do, while the bombs ricocheted through the passages of her brain.

This was the beginning of everything that would mar my mother's life and the lives of those many generations to come.

* * *

The owner of the ammunition factory, where my grandfather Andrzej was an engineer, phoned Gosia, my grandmother, and told her that he was leaving Radom and looking for a safe place to live. He said he would take her and her children wherever she wanted to go, if Andrzej would stay in Radom and take care of the factory. Gosia did not want to leave her husband but felt compelled to leave for the safety of her children.

On the 6th of September, Gosia started packing at midnight. Agata chose to stay with the family, even though, as a Catholic, she would not have been harmed by the Nazis. At 2 a.m., the factory owner arrived with his truck. The two girls and the two women got into the truck and waved at the silhouette of Andrzej, standing at the window in the middle of the night. Agnieszka and Ewa were silent, not understanding what was going on. No one knew if they would ever see Andrzej again.

* * *

Andrzej's boss asked Gosia where she wanted to go. She had decided to go to Lublin, about 100 kilometers east of Radom, where her sister-in-law and mother-in-law lived. On the way there, bombs were falling, and they often had to stop and hide in the woods. They finally arrived safely in Lublin, but that night, the city came under heavy German bombardment.

The next day, Gosia heard from her husband that a few hours after she had left, he departed for Warsaw, eighty kilometers away from Radom, where he had to negotiate with the Ministry of War regarding further deliveries of military equipment. After the meeting, he was preparing to return to Radom, and called the office there, but was told not to return because the German army was there and had taken over the city. He decided instead to get to Lublin and joined thousands of people making an exodus from Warsaw. Everyone seemed to be running away on bikes, cars, trains and foot. The highways were filled with corpses and the smoke of the burning homes was suffocating. Late that night, he arrived safely in Lublin. His children were playing in his sister's house, and he fell to his knees with exhaustion and relief, holding his wife and children, kissing their cheeks.

"Lublin will be targeted in one to two days." Andrzej said grimly, at the dinner table that night. The children were asleep. "Radom was taken quickly by the Germans. One neighboring city after another Hitler is conquering and destroying. Lublin will be next." He paused and looked at his wife whose face was drawn and worried. She was staring at a crumb on the table.

"We should all leave tonight and head to the Romanian border." Gosia sighed.

"You go!" Andrzej's mother said. "I will take care of your wife and daughters. It will be less risky for all. Hitler won't hurt women and children: only men are in danger. Anyhow, the war will be over in a short time."

"I refuse to leave without my family!" Andrzej retorted.

This was the last word. His mother sat quietly and shook her head.

Late that night, the five of them and a neighbor drove to the Romanian border in Andrzej's company car. Agnieszka was asleep in Agata's arms. Ewa quietly looked out of the window, again not knowing what was going on. It was late. She was sleepy. But she could not close her eyes, and she had learned early on never to ask questions.

In Tarnopol, a town sixty kilometers from Lublin, two Polish soldiers stopped them and ordered them to drive off the road onto a field. Then they were told to get out of the car and walk to a nearby village, leaving their car with them for the duration of the war. Andrzej parked the car. There were many other people who also were ordered to vacate their cars. These cars were requisitioned by the Polish army. When the soldiers were busy with other cars and passengers, Andrzej told his family to stay in the car and then he and the neighbor silently lifted the vehicle, turned it in the direction of the highway and then without a sound, they jumped in and with the headlights turned off, Andrzej quickly drove away and raced to the border. The soldiers started shooting at them, but in the darkness, they missed the car.

The next morning, they arrived in Czortków, a town forty kilometers from the Romanian border. It was a sunny day, and fashionably dressed women were sipping tea in coffee houses, unscathed by the horrors from neighboring cities. The car needed repairs, and it was the day before the Jewish New Year, so they decided to spend the night in a hotel while the car was in the garage. The morning after, they got in the car to leave, just as the Russian tanks came into the city. The Russians closed the borders, taking control of the city and all its inhabitants. No one was allowed to leave.

From September 1939 to June 1940, they were forced to live in Czortków, which was now part of Russian- occupied Poland. They all lived in a small room they rented, not sure what was to happen next. After occupying the city, the Russians ordered all engineers to register with them. They needed engineers for rebuilding bridges and other projects. Since he knew some Russian, they immediately hired him to rebuild bombed out bridges in Lwów. He lived there with a cousin, and every weekend went to Czortków to be with his family.

One day, the family went for a walk. They passed through a gate which read, "No Trespassing". Andrzej did not see any guards, so he walked in, and the family followed. Inside was a lovely park with grass and wildflowers. The children began to pick the flowers. Suddenly, two Russian guards appeared out of nowhere, ordered Andrzej to go with them, and told Gosia to go home with the children. They ran home, in terror. Several hours later, Andrzej came home and recounted that they had been suspected of spying on a military installation. The Russians had released him after phoning his employer in Lwów, ascertaining that he worked there as an engineer.

In February 1940, the Russians started deportations to Siberia. The first deportees were Polish citizens in legal and law enforcement professions. In April, they deported wealthy landowners and businessmen. One by one, the Russians uncovered names, finding reason to accuse and deport, to create prisoners from innocent civilians.

At the beginning of May, the Russians demanded that the refugees from the German-occupied part of Poland acquire Russian passports. Andrzej thought they should take them, because if they did not, he thought, the Russians might deport them. Gosia strongly objected. She was not sure why, but intuitively felt it was not the right thing to do.

Despite her grave doubts, they went to the passport office on the last day they were being issued. They arrived at 5:03 pm, and the office was closed at 5pm. They thus did not obtain the Russian passports, and because of this, Andrzej was laid off from his job.

Later, they learned that those who had accepted the passports, though saved from deportation to Siberia, were sent to German concentration camps when the Nazis invaded eastern Poland in July 1941.

One month later, they were indeed deported to Siberia, as part of a mass suspicion of being German spies.

* * *

At midnight on the 28th of June 1940, there was a knock on the door. Earlier that day, Russian authorities had announced that there would be an air raid drill that night, and they ordered everyone in the town to cover their windows so no light would shine through.

In his completely darkened apartment, Andrzej opened the door. Because he had recently lost his job in Lwów, he was home. If entire families were not together that night, they would have been separated.

There were three armed Russian soldiers.

They pointed at Agata. "Who is she?"

"She is my cousin." Andrzej explained.

"She may not come with you."

"Please, officer, she is quiet. She needs to be with us."

The officer looked at her up and down. He nodded.

Had she been left behind, she would have been sent to a prison camp and most certainly would have perished.

"Pack your belongings!" they ordered. They watched every step of the family for the next thirty minutes. Ewa went to the bathroom, and one of the young men followed her and stood at the door with his gun. Home and childhood for Ewa were being ripped away. She had been a nine-year-old with pigtails, floating on a swing, filled with curiosity, and carelessly letting her childhood fly by. Her only curse was being Jewish and Polish in Poland as the Nazis and Russians stormed into the country, and established dominion over it.

As she was crammed into a truck, her present, her future, and her children's and grandchildren's future would be forever dictated. Home, for her, from that night on, meant something you were forced to let go of. Something that was once solid, suddenly became precarious.

Russian voices swirled around her. She didn't understand. She looked at her parents' faces. They were scared. Their faces, laced with fear, settled into her brain, as she remained silent.

There were no windows in the truck. Her two-year-old sister Agnieszka whimpered, and her mother covered her mouth.

Ewa conjured up in her head images of her home in Krakow. The delicate patterns on the sofa's lace she would often trace with her fingertips when she was bored. It soothed her. The wooden banister that curved around like an S. She imagined it was like a snake in the house, one worn smooth by years and years of caressing hands. The sparkle of the chandelier in the dining room, the way the sunlight hit it just right and rainbows flitted across the room. The record player that her father put on every evening, records of Chopin, Beethoven, Brahms. When she was very young, he listened often to Chopin, and she remembered feeling a dreaminess melt her insides with the piano chords. Her mind would go anywhere, she could be anything.

She looked at the dirty walls of the truck. They stunk. She used every ounce of energy she had to fight back the tears.

This was only the beginning of a lifetime of pushing her feelings inside.

* * *

"I have to pee," she whispered to her mother.

Gosia spoke in Russian to the officer.

"My daughter has to urinate."

"There is no time!" he shouted. "We are rescuing you from the Germans! We must hurry!"

Andrzej whispered in his wife's ear in Polish.

"They are not rescuing us. Just you wait."

"But she has to urinate now!" she said to the guard.

Ewa marched in place very fast, while she put her hand on her crotch.

The guard spit on the floor of the truck aiming for her feet. A bit of his slimy saliva landed on her shoe.

He whispered something to the driver who swerved to the side of the road and suddenly stopped. The impact threw Agnieszka onto the floor of the truck. She began to cry. Agata put her hand on the child's mouth and held her tight to her bosom.

In the middle of a field, the armed guard let Ewa out and held a gun to her back as she pulled down her pants. The urine would not come. Visions of her home rapidly left as fear took over. The guard cursed her over and over. She didn't understand the words but understood that she was now a prisoner.

What she would never understand was why.

* * *

In the heart of the night, somewhere in eastern Poland, where the unforgiving skies poured out rain and wind, the truck stopped. A guard opened the door, and with his gun pointed at their backs, he ushered them to a cargo train. Hundreds of other Poles were already packed into the crowded cars, which had one little stove in the middle, and one hole in the floor for a toilet. There were no windows and no light. The stench was suffocating. The stove provided minimal warmth. There were very few coals, not nearly enough to produce enough heat to warm a person from the bitter cold outside. Through cracks between the boards, they could tell day from night. Twice a day the door opened, and they were given some soup and bread. Their main concern was trying to find out which direction the train was going because they had no idea where they were being taken.

They would be on that train for more than two weeks.

Everyone on the train had had a life. Everyone on that train was now a prisoner with no explanation. Hitler would have murdered them mercilessly. Stalin wanted to eliminate them.

The sounds inside deafened Ewa. Many people were crying. Those who were not crying were singing. Some sang bawdy love songs, the lyrics of which she would remember some eighty years later, when dementia had ravaged her brain.

Chapter Three

My mother's childhood stories of war and deportation were our dinnertime entertainment. We listened to them while eating our American Hamburger Helper dinners and frozen peas, the latter of which we hated. For us to eat our vegetables, she told us to consume them one by one. Each pea represented a member of the family, many of whom had perished in the war. But this was all a game, and her tales were just stories without sentiment, without tears, without a punch that would cause any distress for her beloved family. This was her country now, her beloved country.

The U.S.A., however, meant nothing to me as a child. It was just where I was born. I had no attachment to it, no sense of pride in being an American. However, we all loved watching the Olympic games every few years. The Americans kept winning medals, and in the American culture, we were taught at an early age that we were supposed to love the fact that our people swept up most of the medals, especially the gold. Each time an athlete won an event, they played the Star-Spangled Banner. As we sat, glued to the TV, my mother cried. It was the only time, except when my grandfather died, that my mother shed a tear.

"Why are you crying?" I would ask her every two years when American after American seemed to be winning. The Mark Spitz Summer Olympics of 1968 and 1972 produced more tears for her than any other year of my childhood.

"Because it is very moving for me."

That was one of her favorite expressions, whose vagueness only made me more confused. In my youth and adolescence I was never smart enough to read between the lines, to understand even a little bit why this song that highlighted bombs bursting in the air would have such a positive impact on my mother, the person who let me sit on her lap and who was always there for me, who let me be a child, who let me live in a land of innocence much longer than most kids my age.

This land of innocence that she spread around us so freely was, of course, infinitely wrapped around the expectation that I would do no wrong, that I would have no feelings, except those of happiness. There didn't seem to be any other options. The problem was the older I got, the less I understood the path to happiness. But mostly, it just didn't fit into the family's pattern of things, which was laden with undisclosed tension. I was so caught up in the nebulousness of it all, that I could not even fathom that my mother had survived trauma. I couldn't even begin to imagine what that might look like.

One day when I was in the sixth grade, a Jewish classmate gave an oral book report on *Mein Kampf*. He was shaking as he read it. I did not understand what he was talking about. I didn't know why he was quivering. I thought maybe he was sick, or something was wrong with him, and I focused on the strange clothes he was wearing. He was wearing a suit that day, and I wondered why he was wearing a suit to school. When I came home, I wanted to ask my mother who was Hitler, but she wasn't home, and later, I forgot about my question and continued with my uninquisitive life.

Our television viewing was censored. The only shows she allowed my two sisters and me to view were The Brady Bunch and The

Partridge Family. The movies we saw were all G rated, and once again, happy. Our dinnertime conversations alluded to the fact that she had survived and survived and survived, but her survival stories were like Disney films, encapsulated in an emotionless void. Eating our peas was more important to her than us trying to understand the implications of her emotionless stories.

Chapter Four

For the next several years of her young life, Ewa lived in places that barely housed her. Home had been irretrievably stolen from her. During those formative years she had to erase the very concept of home from her memory. Survival, which was now the theme, meant a sudden purging of something primal to the human system.

The train arrived in Siberia, near a small town called Tavda, in the province of Sverdlosk. It was the summer, however the cold wind from the arctic blew incessantly. There were very few forms of life, and no trees. The sky rarely changed hues from grey to grey.

In one month, Ewa's childhood had vanished. Before that knock on the door, she was full of hope, full of joy. Before the war, she learned how to ride a bicycle, swim, ice skate, and ski, all from her father's lessons. She and her father would ride their bicycles out into the country together, laughing and loving being away from the rest of the family. Back at home, she and her father played games together and he made her doll furniture out of old postcards.

* * *

One day, when they first arrived, she asked her father a question. She was cold. Her clothes smelled of urine. Her hair was infested with lice from the journey in the filthy train.

"Why are we here?"

Her father was silent. He was like an ox that would save the family from destruction over and over, but he had no words to tell his eldest daughter.

"Ask your mother," was all he could say. Then he walked away. His stern face grew sterner with each passing moment in the Gulag.

"Why are we here?" Ewa persisted, looking at her mother's face, seeing more worry lines in it than ever.

"There is no answer, Ewunia."

"There must be an answer." Ewa's face scrunched up. Every emotion was hidden in the folds of her face.

Her mother sighed. No words came out.

Ewa walked outside. The barren world around her smothered all answers. One of her duties was to get bread for the family, an item often in short supply. She had to wait in a long line before the store opened. Repeatedly she was pushed and knocked down by larger, stronger adults. Usually, she would arrive home empty- handed. If she did manage to obtain a loaf of bread, someone would steal it from her hands. Often, she held back tears.

She had met a girl on the cattle car. Her name was Danuta. They both had baby sisters named Agnieszka. Danuta was built like a cow, and never dreamed of lace on sofas. Her family's hut was about ten meters away. One day, not wanting to go home and show her family that they would not have bread for another week, she knocked on Danuta's door. Her mother answered. She had been crying. Danuta's grandmother had gotten sick on the train and the guards had pushed her dead body off into the Russian tundra.

"Why are we here?" Ewa persisted, looking in Danuta's eyes.

"Because the Russians hate the Poles. Because Stalin is pretending to be friends with Hitler, and they all hate us. Because it is war. Stalin, actually, despises Hitler, but they have one thing in common: they need to get rid of people and treat them like rats. War gives them an excuse to do whatever they want."

Ewa nodded. She didn't know if what Danuta was saying was true, but at least someone had an answer to her question. At least someone had words.

"What do we do here? We can't even run away. There's no place to go."

"We do as they say. We will get used to it. If we don't, we will die like poisoned cockroaches."

Somehow that made Ewa laugh.

"I saw some railroad tracks. Let's follow them and see where they go."

Ewa nodded. Danuta's mother and her sister were both crying. Her father was gone. Fathers were taken first and had to begin carrying logs for the sawmills. Mothers and children would start the next day. No one would be spared. Even babies and toddlers would be told what to do for Mother Russia. "Who doesn't work, doesn't eat" was their motto.

Danuta and Ewa hid in the forest.

"Don't make a sound!" Danuta whispered. "There are guards everywhere. We are not supposed to go anywhere without a pass. If they see us, they will tell our parents and will give us harder jobs for a whole month. They will also reduce the food rations for the whole family." She looked around her. "I think this way goes to the railway tracks."

"How do you know?" Ewa whispered. Danuta seemed to know everything.

"I saw it from the train last week as we arrived."

Ewa never noticed things like that. Her eyesight was quite poor. It would not be until she was twenty years old that the doctors discovered she had a severe case of astigmatism.

They walked on listening to the silence. Nothing lived in Siberia. Ewa had the feeling that she had stepped into the world of the dead. She looked down at her feet. She always looked down when she walked. Her father always looked ahead. Danuta did both.

"Look!" she whispered. "There they are." Her eyes pointed to the left. Rusted metal in straight lines went on for miles, an infinity of train tracks.

"We are outside the limits of the camp, I think. The guards won't find us here." Danuta still whispered.

They followed the tracks, their footsteps even and matched. Minutes, hours, passed, and nothing seemed to matter except for those moments when they felt free, when there were no borders, and no hatred between humans.

Chapter Five

I never felt like I belonged anywhere when I was a teenager. I floated in and out of the misfit group, a motley gathering of girls, who, for one reason or another, did not want to be part of the mainstream, or were being pushed away from it. I thought I was there for the former reason, but looking back, I was there for the latter. My older sister tried to be popular, but the well-liked girls told her, point blank, that she couldn't fit in with their elitist group because our mother came from another country and had an accent.

People used to tell me my mother had a strong accent. I never detected a thing. My mother was perfect. She had no accent. No trauma. Nothing unusual. I loved her more than anyone else on the planet. If I could, I would push everyone else away and live on a small island with just my mother.

But something inside me told me it was impossible. Society advised me I was supposed to be my own person and separate from my mother. I figured that meant I needed to leave for a while. My oldest sister had been an exchange student when she was my age, so I decided to do the same. I really wanted to go to France, as I had been learning French in school, but my mother didn't want me to live so far away. So, instead, I went to New Jersey. I lived with another family. The parents insisted I call them Mom and Dad. They didn't have accents; they weren't Jewish, and they didn't have this unnamed hovering trauma zooming over their heads. I told my parents I was happy there, but in truth, I was miserable. I had no friends, and I missed my real mother. My exchange student sister resented me to the point of hatred because I was sweet and obedient, and she was mean and argumentative, and her parents liked me more. My mother missed me. She wondered why I was across the country. I wondered that too.

"Why do you feel the need to run away from your family, Helen, when you have a good family right here in this house?" she asked me one day on the phone.

I didn't have an answer for her.

The next day it snowed. Flecks of white danced through the sky like fairy princesses. I was at school, looking out the window, thinking only of dancing frozen fairies, when the loudspeaker blared.

"Due to the rapidly worsening weather, school is now closed for the next few days. Please go to your assigned bus immediately. Repeat. School is now closed for the next few days. Please go to your assigned bus immediately."

Everyone around me was abuzz. I got caught in the frenzy as I threw on my winter coat and made my way outside. The blizzard encompassed me and sent a chill through me. At first, I was happy. Everyone around me was, so I figured that was the way to feel. Dozens of yellow school buses quickly left, one by one. The large tires sloshed through the rapidly amassing snow. I thought of my mother as the other kids laughed and bonded, as they overlooked me, as everyone always overlooked me. I had my violin with me. We were supposed to have orchestra practice that day.

The bus arrived at my street. I stepped out into a frozen world. It smelled like death somehow. The stillness was eerie. I had never stepped into a blizzard, and the sensations were ethereal, and quite destabilizing. By the time I arrived at my house, I had to pee like crazy. I put my violin in the dry garage and ran to the back door. It didn't occur to me that everyone in the family would be arriving soon, that a snow day means that everyone needs to be home and off the roads.

As I was washing my hands, relieved, I heard a loud sound. The garage door was opening. The car, driven by my exchange mother, drove in.

"Oh no!" I yelled. My voice didn't normally get that loud.

I ran to the garage, listening to the crunch of tires on finely crafted wood.

I was shivering. Trying to hold back tears. I could not speak as I grabbed a broom, took the handle, stuck it under the car and pushed out the case.

I have never opened it. It was like the disheveled corpse of everything that had gone wrong in my family's history, everything that had no words, that was hidden in the black violin case.

The next week I was on the plane. The semester exchange period was over, and I was returning home.

Chapter Six

The incessant snow and ice seeped into every pore. There was nothing but extreme cold in Siberia, so much so that everything felt numb and could never thaw.

Gosia stared out the window at the bleak world. She was on the tenth day of a hunger strike. She had refused to do manual labor, so the commandant had put her in the camp prison: a room with a bench and a miniscule window, more like a slit in the wood, yet big enough to let in a constant blast of cold. She had told him she would not eat until she was given permission to abstain from the hard physical work her body was not meant to do.

"I will not cave into such nonsense!" he retorted. "I don't care what your *bourgeois* imaginings tell you can or can't do. You will work, or you will die here. And if you die here, we will throw your body out in the snow." He smirked. "One less body to feed that way." Then he locked the door to the room, took the key, and stormed out.

Gosia sat on the bench and stared outside. After her beloved mother died from dysentery when Gosia was eighteen years old, she learned to become like a stone, to not cry, to not show emotions, and instead, to be a warrior and fight for what was right. Justice was her guide in most everything she did.

* * *

She was the only woman to receive a PhD from the University of Vienna in 1929. She was very pregnant with her first child. Ewa kicked hard the day of the hooding ceremony. Being a professor was more important than being a parent, and she fought hard for the former to happen. Getting pregnant was unfortunately easy to do, and she ignored her pregnancy until a few weeks before the birth. The day the baby came out, Gosia thought her life was over. She had no maternal instincts, and she had no desire to learn how to develop them.

She had hired a nursemaid who eventually became a full-time nanny for Ewa. Agata took on the role of mother, and she surrounded the little girl's life with an abundance of love, attention, and play. She allowed the child to roam and to dream, and she was always there for her with adoration and respect.

Agata, a poor, widowed, peasant, had a five-year-old son of her own, with a mental disability, who stayed with Agata's mother while she took loving care of the child who was not her own. She spent more time with Ewa than her own son. The day her employer's family was taken away from their home and deported, Agata volunteered to go with them. There were now two children: Ewa and her little sister, Agnieszka, who was born in 1937.

"But what about your own child?" Gosia asked. She paced the floor, throwing things in suitcases, and then throwing them out. The guard was at the door, telling them they had fifteen minutes.

Agata was silent. She looked away, hiding her tears. There was no time for anything. There was no time to see her mother and say good-bye to her child.

"Who will look after your children?" Agata exclaimed. She did not mention her son. She never did. She never talked about him. It was like there was a strange void between the child she carried and herself. Still, the pain of leaving him was almost too much to bear. Her feet wobbled, she could barely stand, and she had to sit down for a minute. The guard walked by with a scowl, and she immediately rose and motioned for Gosia to sit down while she finished the packing.

That brief, hardly noticeable minute was the only time she showed to the family how she really felt.

* * *

As always, Agata was spot on. She knew the sisters needed her, and maybe she needed them too.

With Agata to look after the children, Gosia bloomed in her work as a professor of German Literature at the University. Her passion for teaching was unsurpassed, and each semester there were endless waiting lists of students who wanted to get into her classes. Her favorite genre was German expressionism, and many of her courses focused on the work of Kafka, translated, and Nietzsche. She was a defiant rebel in her life, and her teaching encompassed a rebellion of the mind. She loved being at the center of intellectual curiosity, and often hosted soirees deep into the night with fellow professors, but mostly with graduate students who savored her soliloquies, savoring every one of her words.

One day, this glamorous world came to a halt.

"We must move to Radom," Andrzej announced one day at dinner, early in the summer of 1939. The children were playing outside with Agata. Ewa, radiant after a successful teaching year that just finished its term, stared hard at her husband.

"Why?"

"It's not safe here anymore in the west." He paused. "Hitler is advancing."

Gosia had learned over the years that when her husband said things, usually they were true. When he said things, usually there was no point in arguing. They simply were the new fact. He did give her space for all her intellectual pursuits. On top of everything, theirs was a beautiful match. As independent as she was, he was her rock, and she depended on him to make major decisions for the family.

She nodded her head. "Why Radom?"

"The supervisor of my company has begged me to move there immediately. He will oversee everything to make things smooth for you... and for us. I need to be there very early tomorrow. You, the children, and Agata will arrive next week to settle into the new apartment he has found for our family."

"What makes you think Radom is safe?"

"Rumor has it that the Russians will occupy the east. They are safer than the Germans."

"But Radom isn't that far from Krakow."

"If we must leave Radom, we will. But for now, Radom is safe."

He held her hand and looked in her eyes.

"We will be together. That is the most important thing."

She nodded. Usually, she had many words to say. That evening, there were none as she   watched her husband get up to leave, heading to the bedroom to pack his suitcase.

Ewa ran in, her face flushed. She had something in her hand that she held out. She beamed.

"Daddy, Daddy! Look what I found outside with Agata!"

"Not now, Ewunia."

She looked at his face. It was more severe than usual.

"Can we build bridges later?" Ewa loved to play that game with her father. He mostly did the building, and she would watch him. He called it "building bridges with Daddy". He would get so excited and happy when he did this, as if he were still a child.

"Not now, Ewunia. Go find your mother. Maybe you can show her what you are holding in your hands."

Ewa had been taught not to notice things. She did not see that he had packed a suitcase with all the family's valuables inside and very few clothes.

* * *

Gosia looked out the window from her prison cell, watching the snow fall, feeling its cold seep into her skull. She barely remembered her past, the accolades she had received, and the attention that regularly serenaded her life as a professor. She hadn't seen her family for ten days, and she began to wonder if she might never see them again. As her mind drifted away from the prison walls into nothingness and the snow continued its relentless fall across the vast landscape, she closed her eyes and let any dreams she once had vanish beneath her lids. Now, all was nothingness, an infinite barrage of nothingness in an infinitely hostile land.

Chapter Seven

When I returned from New Jersey, I was even more depressed. I had placed the unopened violin case with its shattered contents against the wall in my bedroom and pushed my nightstand in front of it where I couldn't see it. I felt even more lost than before I left. I didn't have words to describe anything I was experiencing, as if a nebulousness was surrounding me. My mother would come to my room and look at me with a helpless expression on her face. There was, however, a bond between us, an unspoken message of uncertainty. Neither of us could name our struggle. Neither of us could even say the word struggle out loud. Happiness was our only choice, and there was no option for any other experience. I developed a saying for this uncertainty, this not happy discomforting feeling that had no detour: "googy". I was "googy" all the time in those days. I imagined not being on this planet. I imagined it often. Since I couldn't attain happiness, and since my only state was "googiness", I wanted to flee my existence.

During this time, my father suggested we look for another violin.

If my mother was disconnected from any feeling and could not express what was really going on with her, my father, Arthur, was worse. He, too, was surviving trauma, but his was familial. His mother hated all men, beginning with her ex-husband, and ending with her own son. Her husband had walked out on the family. In her rage, she told my father over and over that he was disgusting and would never amount to anything; that only his sister would do anything significant in life.

I had looked at pictures of my father when he was a young child. He was dressed as a girl, and he looked like a doll. He had a preciousness in him, a fragile face that asked for tenderness. No one in his life provided this. His sister was given ammunition by their mother to hate him. The more she did, the more she got praised. My father developed a severe speech impediment, and it wasn't until a teacher pulled him aside in high school and told him there was a speech therapist who could help him, that he began to function in the world. He had no friends throughout his childhood. His abusive sister was his only companion. She wanted to become a teacher, so he decided to become a teacher. He never asked himself if this was really what he wanted to do.

When the U.S. government called for men to enlist in the Army to serve in the Korean War, he signed up. Just before he left for basic training, he met my mom. She had tuberculosis and was knitting sweaters in a sanatorium. A mutual friend, a former classmate, had told him to meet her. She was a nurse-intern at the sanatorium.

From Berkeley, he took three buses to the brick building in the woods, and encountered my mother, emaciated, lost, knitting and undergoing painful treatments that would forever damage her lungs.

My father had never been on a date, didn't know a thing about women and thought they all hated men, especially him.

But my mother didn't hate him. On the contrary she liked him, mainly because he wasn't afraid of all her baggage. Unable to express her feelings, she couldn't really say what she felt when a man, a handsome one, stood before her, unperturbed by her illness, her foreignness, her thick accent, her Jewishness, her awkwardness in a maimed world.

Their lives were derived from trauma, but they could not express this shared pain.

He went to war and wrote to her. She wrote back, the only letters he received as he witnessed death all around him. Two years later, he returned. She was no longer sick. He proposed to her, and she said yes. They did not speak of pain. They did not bring up the past, except in stories that did not address the morose aspects of their lives. They were happy.

My father had no idea how to address, how to understand pain. Somehow, he was able to simplify the human condition, to let his brain wrap itself around the tangibly happy moments in life. My parents were a perfect match.

* * *

Like my mother, my father had no idea what my depression was about, but he did know that I didn't own a violin anymore. Every Saturday for a month, he and I took the train across the bay to San Francisco violin shops. We returned each time with four violins, one in each hand, which I would try out and present to my violin teacher. She would listen to each one and reject the choices. So, the next Saturday, we would bring them back and gather four more. Finally, at the end of the month, I found my violin. My teacher approved. The instrument had a sonority that surpassed all the others. While my parents helped with the cost, I paid for some of it with my own money, saved from my weekly allowance and the funds I gathered from babysitting neighborhood kids.

As I held the violin to my chin, on the day it was finally mine, I decided that I might never know how the world worked, or make a friend, or ever leave the googy state I was in, but with my violin I would create my own universe. I might not understand trauma and I might

not even be able to use the word for decades, but my violin and I could
be partners through the miasma of unspoken, complicated tragedies
that seemed to be inherent in the human condition.

Chapter Eight

While her mother was incarcerated, Ewa spent more time than ever with her new friend Danuta. She called her "the ox" because there was nothing that she was unable to do. She revered her and her perseverance against all odds. She admired her stoicism and vowed to adopt the same manner. Danuta was able to couple this philosophy with an adventurous spirit. She didn't need to be a rebel, but in essence everything she did was seditious. After their workload was done, they went every day to the train tracks. Some days, they met gypsies along the tracks. As their homes were collapsible, they often wouldn't be there the next day. Danuta and Ewa would fill their pockets with objects from their former lives, items their mothers had stashed in their suitcase before they left. Soaps and handkerchiefs, fancy underwear and gloves, they gave to the gypsies in exchange for food. Somehow, they always had potatoes, onions and bread, so the trade made all parties satisfied. They were always hungry in Siberia and did anything they could to get food.

"Why is your mother in prison anyway?" Danuta asked one day, when they were away from the camp border and free to talk.

"She refused to work."

"Why?"

"It was too hard for her." Ewa paused. "She is a professor."

Danuta nodded. "My mother is a lawyer."

There was silence after that.

The next day Ewa went to Danuta's barrack after work.

She did her usual knock. One loud, three quiet raps on the door.

There was no answer.

She tried again, and still there was no answer.

She opened the door, and looked in.

"Danuta?" she called out.

Silence.

She entered and saw the remains of a family that had disappeared. There were piles of dust on the floor, crumbs in the corner of the one room they all lived in, mouse droppings, but otherwise everything was gone.

Ewa shook her head, attempting to hold back the tears that were on the verge of being shed. *She was the best friend I ever had.*

She looked around again, wondering if maybe there was a note hidden for her somewhere; she wondered where they went.

She stepped outside, feeling an ache in her heart, an absence of something that had once fluttered in the breeze, which was gone now.

I loved her.

She quickly brushed away her feelings, as she walked to the railroad tracks. She knew the path by heart now and in her mind, she recalled all the conversations she had had with Danuta over the past few months, all the words of wisdom her friend had passed on to her. She had learned a lot, about so many things, from this girl who had walked into her life quite by chance and had left just as suddenly.

Did they escape this prison? She wondered. *And if so, how?*

She tried to remember every conversation they had, and if there was any mention of this idea of escape.

No, not a word about it, she decided.

A gypsy, a boy about five years old, approached her with his hand out. He pointed to his family and motioned that they had food to trade. In the past month, Ewa had begun to learn Russian to make these exchanges. She moved towards the adults, reaching in her pockets for a pair of silk stockings she had taken from her mother's pile. She wondered why her mother had packed, of all things, silk stockings, before being captured and taken to the worst corner of the world. But in this case, it proved to be very lucrative.

While trading with one of the elders, a greying woman with no teeth, the old woman spoke:

"So sad, your friend."

"Do you know what happened?" Ewa was shaking.

"Last night. It was late."

"What? What happened?"

"They were running along the tracks late last night. Your friend. Baby in mother's arms."

Then there was something she said Ewa couldn't understand.

"What happened to her and her family, and where was their father?"

"Father was not there. Your friend, and mother and baby. They shot them."

Ewa gulped. Her face turned white.

She dropped the stockings, stuffed the potatoes in her pockets, and ran.

She ran into the woods, ran in circles around the trees, ran until she got dizzy and then she collapsed and pounded the earth. She pounded hard, over, and over as she felt her tears fall.

She cried hard, big drops of water that sunk into the roots of the trees.

It was the only time in her non-infant life that she cried. Except for the Olympics, she didn't cry again until her father died thirty-five years later.

Chapter Nine

I was never very good at the violin, but that didn't seem to matter. My instrument became an extension of myself regardless. It could express things that I otherwise could not. I practiced several hours a day and lost myself in the world of Mozart, Beethoven, Handel, and Brahms. I played in my high school orchestra, and in a local youth symphony.

While my mother continued to tell us the harrowing stories of her life, as if they belonged to the benign world, I had sunk into an even deeper abyss. I closed the door to my bedroom and jumbled together those unnamed emotions with the soul of my instrument, the latter of which allowed me to transcend absolutely anything.

My violin also brought me to Alyssa.

A year older, Alyssa, with unruly curls and an infinitely gorgeous violin, came into my life and made me swoon. She was the concert-mistress in the high school orchestra, and when she played, visions of perfection would flood my mind. In her junior year, she performed *The Lark Ascending* by Vaughn Williams that left me breathless. Not only was her interpretation of this stunning piece flawless, but her playing exuded such a fecundity of the instrument. I remember sitting in the middle of the second violin section and feeling like I could fly away, be anyone, if only to hear her play on that piece of wood. She held every note with a breath of sweetness, intensity, a passion that experienced no borders.

Alyssa did not talk to me that year. I am not even sure she knew I existed. I admired her in my private moments and hoped one day she might see me.

When she was in her senior year, and I was in my junior, I developed a plan. I spoke of it with the conductor of the orchestra and my violin teacher, and they both agreed.

I would play *the Mozart violin concerto #3* with the high school orchestra. Every day I practiced and practiced, and my hands became the vehicle for notes that soared out of me. I knew I would never be perfect, and I knew I would never be able to play like Alyssa, but that knowledge did not stop me from my determination to create music and to create something in my life that was meaningful. Mozart was not Vaughn Williams. His music was light and frivolous. I was not mature enough to express the deeper sentiments of life. I was an unconscious, unawake being who barely knew day from night, but still I was a musician.

My violin teacher was heroic. She made me believe I could really perform this piece, and she worked hard with me. Midway into the year, the reality hit: I was doing it. I was getting ready to perform in front of an audience of more than a hundred people. In my quiet moments, I giggled to myself at my audacity.

Working on this concerto also allowed Alyssa to notice me, as the entire orchestra was rehearsing the score.

That made me pause.

She didn't say much. She just smiled. She could have been condescending. She was infinitely superior as a musician. But that was not what she was expressing in her smile. Rather, it encouraged me to play, to perform, to sweep myself into the music, as she had done.

On the evening of the performance, I was naturally filled with anxiety. In the rehearsal room, she came up to me, and pinned a rose corsage on my dress.

"Play beautifully, darling!" she said quietly to me. I felt so nervous, so gangly in my approach to life and to music. But in that moment, as I smelled the rose on my chest and looked into her eyes as I thanked her, I felt that if there was ever an antidote to what I had experienced in my life, it was now.

She walked away, and although I didn't know it at the time, I would never speak to her again.

I went onstage, my violin tucked under my arm. I looked out at the audience but couldn't see anyone in the vast sea of faces. I knew my family was there: my parents, my sister, my grandmother. My violin teacher was in the audience as well. The concert hall was packed.

I turned to the oboist, a girl in my group of misfits. She played an "A" in perfect pitch as the orchestra tuned. I took a whiff of the rose that exuded an intoxicating fragrance, I looked up at the conductor, and I began. Everything I practiced flew out of my fingers. Mozart would have been happy.

Then, at the end of the third and last movement, as I began the cadenza, my mind went blank, my fingers froze on the fingerboard, and I looked at my violin and didn't know what to do. I looked up at the conductor and he tried to get me back on track, but I couldn't hear him. Instead, I heard gunshots, I heard bombs, I heard the cries from ancestors, wails in an unforgiving night sky. I felt like I was being drawn into some force that was beyond me, beyond the violin, beyond anything I could imagine.

I wanted to bolt from the stage. I was done with this ridiculous concerto.

The orchestra was silent. They were staring at me. I didn't glance at the audience, but I sensed they were watching me. I looked up at the conductor once again, and he had such a warm smile on his face, while his mouth formed the notes of what I needed to play next. The guns, the bombs and the wails in my head became silent as my fingers unfroze, my bow arm moved up and down the fingerboard, and my brain danced in tandem.

I finished the cadenza. I played it more beautifully than I had ever played it. The orchestra came in at the end, and together we laid the concerto to rest.

* * *

I never understood why the cries emerged and the bombs crashed in the middle of my performance. After the concert was over, my family celebrated my accomplishment, and I fell back into a state of exhausted numbness.

The next day was the last day of school for the year.

On the day after, I went to get the mail and, in the box, not post-marked, was an envelope with a peacock feather attached to the outside.

"Dearest Helen," it began. I shivered with this introduction.

The letter went on for eight pages. In it, Alyssa poured out her feelings of love for a man she had just met and would be joining in Texas. My mailbox was her last stop before this adventure.

In the middle of her hand-written epistle, she told me that one day, I will find my place of greatness if I just allow myself to follow the path of passion. She wrote that when she placed the rose on my dress, she saw in my eyes an innocence begging for expression, a child in the world of the artist, a child who loved, who is open, and who was ripe for the embodiment of the creative soul. She urged me to never stop playing music, to let my violin be my guide.

I read this letter ten times, and then I hid it away somewhere, and never found it again. I tried to find Alyssa. I looked up her name in the directory. I wanted to talk to her. I wanted to see her again. For several years, this was my quest. Finally, decades later, with the internet as my guide, I discovered she had a daughter and contacted her.

In a one sentence email, she said that Alyssa had killed herself two years earlier.

Chapter Ten

Gosia, emaciated and withering, pleaded with the camp commandant one last time.

"I have two young children who need their mother."

"Then go to work. And you will see your children at the end of
the day."

"But I will die if I do the work you have prescribed for me."

"You are dying of starvation anyway, stupid woman."

Gosia knew he was trying to break her, humiliate her. This had been
his tactic for the past two weeks.

"Do you have a wife?" She had never asked this. In her mostly demented and starving state, she sensed this would break him.

His tough, hardened face shifted. He went from a mean man to a
vulnerable child.

"She died."

"When?"

"A year ago. Right before I was stationed in Siberia."

"I am sorry to hear this. You loved her very much."

"More than the moon."

He opened his mouth to say more, but then caught himself.

"Oh, leave me alone."

He took his collection of keys and opened the door to her cell. "Now, leave me alone. I never want to see you again."

* * *

Gosia returned home late that night. The children were asleep, and her husband was sitting at the table staring at a map. There was a tiny sliver of light that came from a rickety string attached to the ceiling. He looked up, smiled and ran over to her holding her tight in his arms.

"Kochanie!"

She sank into his chest as he held her up. She was so weak that had he not held her, she would have collapsed to the floor. He took her hand, led her to the table and tore off a stale piece of bread. She devoured it in one gulp and then he gave her more. He had her sip some water.

She began to tell him the tactic that saved her life.

Andrzej laughed. "Here's to the dead wife." He held up his glass.

She laughed.

"Look what arrived at the door an hour before you arrived."

He handed her an envelope.

She opened it.

Inside were exit permits for the family, including Agata.

"That's how I knew you would be coming home soon."

He kissed her on the cheek and led her to bed, holding her close to him tighter than he ever had.

Chapter Eleven

My mother always referred to my father as the "knight in shining armor" who arrived in her life and rescued her from her past.

One of the few times she alluded to any pain in her past was in a story she told often, which, for me, became a metaphor for her life. When she was still young in Poland, she had a little friend who was Catholic, named Marysia. One December the two of them were in the woods with Marysia's older brother. He had an axe with him and together they chopped down a small tree that they were going to bring inside their house for Christmas. My mother was entranced by this idea and asked the brother if he would cut one down for her to bring home. He did happily and after that they went to my mother's house when her parents were out and set up the tree in the living room.

That evening, her father came home from work and saw the tree.

Without saying a word, he picked up the tree and threw it out the window, far away from the house. Then he got some matches and some paper, and as he watched the flames envelop the tree, he screamed out.

"Don't you ever bring a tree into our home!" he screamed. "Wait until your mother finds out. This is a Jewish house, and trees are not brought into Jewish homes in December."

Then he stormed off.

My mother, from that point on, told herself: *"the first moment I can,*

I will have a Christmas tree. And I will put it prominently inside my home."

And she never forgot that pledge. My parents got married in November. One month later, they bought a tree, and decorated it. Together they forged a new life, and without putting words to their legacy of traumas, they found happiness.

But in this outward expression of freedom, my mother's soul must have carried within it a longing that never died, a mourning for what was. She was different and because of this, she must have realized at an early age there were extreme consequences. Had the war never occurred, had her days of carefree swinging and her pigtails sailing in the wind been allowed to follow their natural path, had she been able to leave her parents' home when she decided, home would have been entirely different. Home would have mattered on a completely distinct level, allowing her to find stability every day, in the opening and closing of doors, at will, letting in the light as she chose.

But none of this, of course, was ever expressed. They say that like meets like. Both my parents had this in common: a home forever shifting.

As my parents produced three children...daughters...in seven years, my father changed jobs every other year. By the time I was seven, I had five homes, and before I was born, my parents had four more. Packing and moving, uprooting oneself from that which gives you nourishment and stability, had become a pattern for them.

For me, home was just a place. Nothing in my parents' house ever changed position after we moved the last time when I was seven. The couch never budged an inch. The chairs were placed in certain corners and stayed there. The curtains were always drawn, never letting light in, to prevent the fading of the furniture which never moved. The windows opened and closed, as did the doors, letting air in, and us out, yet there was a constant feeling of stagnancy in that design, in the sense that rootedness was not only taking place, but it was from a tree that was badly damaged. A rooted, ill, tree only produces ill-forming branches.

Throughout my teenage years, I felt that in that house, there was a continual stifling of the spirit within those walls. Many fights occurred between my parents and my sisters and me. There was so much tension that ripened in that place like an unchecked mold. The happy world that was supposed to be, in fact, kept showing signs of the opposite.

My mother claimed she loved this home. For her, it seemed to symbolize permanence in a life where permanence was stolen from her. It was a place where she never had to express all the rage she encountered before and from the day she was carted away.

She lived in a home that was able to cover it all up, or so she believed.

However, inside of me was this nagging feeling that vaguely described what happened on a dark night in the middle of Poland decades ago, affirming the notion that history stays inside a soul, generations later; without using the word trauma, trauma insidiously continued to wave its ugly head.

Chapter Twelve

The first evacuation of Poles from Siberia began in Krasnovodsk, U.S.S.R., and eventually ended in Bandar Pahlavi, Iran which was then controlled by the Soviets.

In June 1941 Germany began an unexpected attack on Russia. Suddenly, Russia realized it needed more allies, so they agreed to release the Polish citizens they had imprisoned. Stalin wanted to create an army from these prisoners to fight against the Germans. On the 30th of July 1941 he accepted a proposal from Polish General Sikorski to allow the Poles to leave Siberia. He appointed General Wladyslaw Anders (who had just been released from prison in Moscow) to be the commander-in-chief of this army which would be under British command. Stalin wanted to get this army in action right away, but Anders told him to wait because the Poles were ill and exhausted from two years of forced labor.

In the early spring of 1942, Stalin declared a one-time amnesty for Polish citizens in Russia. The Prime Minister of Poland, Sikorski, and the Soviet Ambassador to the United Kingdom, Mayski, signed a treaty that would last for only a few months. Polish General Anders was ordered to evacuate thousands of Polish citizens who had been arrested by the Soviets. The Polish army led some of them to the train station where they would travel to Samarkand, Uzbekistan. 90% of these citizens were Catholic and there was a handful of Polish Jews who were granted amnesty. About 10,000 Polish citizens were

released from the 1.7 million captured by the Russians. There were two evacu-
ations, one in March for one week and one in August that lasted three weeks.
There were no other departures and in early January of the next year Stalin
revoked the agreement. Most of the remaining Poles perished in the Gulag.

The Polish consulate in Russia issued temporary passports for the evacuees
who all headed south amidst terrible conditions. Many people froze to death,
starved, or died of typhoid and dysentery during this transport, as hygiene was
abominable. Those who walked this journey often did not make it.

The ones who survived arrived in army reception camps in Tashkent,
Samarkand, Kermine, and Ashkhabad, Uzbekistan. Those who were healthy
enlisted in the Polish army. Some were selected and given food and shelter. The
hundreds of thousands of civilians who were not selected, including women and
children, were forced to camp outside the army bases. The heat was suffocat-
ing, dysentery, typhus, and scarlet fever spread and killed many of the refugees.

* * *

The manager of the sawmill quickly found out that Andrzej's wife had obtained the coveted exit permits for the family. He called him into his office and tried to bribe him into staying. He offered him caviar, ham and liqueurs of the finest quality, items that were reserved for only the highest level of Communist Party officials. He warned Andrzej that the hot and humid conditions and the fatal rampant diseases in Uzbekistan could instantly kill his wife and children.

"We are leaving," Gosia announced, the night Andrzej presented her with the two choices.

"But what if we wait until the Siberian winter is over? It has already almost begun; the ground is already frozen."

"We are leaving now. If we wait, we may never leave Siberia."

The next day, Andrzej presented Gosia with a piece of paper that indicated he had given notice at work, and they would be leaving in two weeks, in the first week of September.

Gosia's fears were unerring. Two days after they left, no one was allowed to exit the camp anymore.

* * *

On a very cold morning on the sixth of September 1942, Ewa, Agnieszka, their parents and Agata, started on foot out of Siberia. A light early autumn snow fell. Only Agnieszka looked back for a brief second at the prison gates that were now open. The rest of the family looked forward, watching their steps so they wouldn't slip and fall on the icy ground in front of them.

They trudged through frozen land. Their shoes, which were never meant to survive the icy Gulag, slid on the ice. They walked in silence in the direction of the train station. Andrzej held their suitcase that contained their lives condensed into one box with flimsy latches.

Their faces were drawn into an expression of uncertainty. They had all been released from prison and had no idea where they would be going next. Home, for them, was only a distant memory of a place that no longer existed, that once housed their joys and sorrows, but was now infinitely unreachable. Somehow, they knew they would never be able to return to Poland.

"It's because of the letter I wrote to Stalin," Gosia said quietly to her husband as they walked farther away from the gulag gates.

"What letter?"

"In my prison cell, I had to do something. My mind was going in terrible directions, and I imagined every day I might never see you again."

Andrzej stared at her as he walked. "What letter?" He persisted in

49

a muffled voice so the children wouldn't hear.

"I was able to obtain some paper and a pencil, and I wrote to Stalin."

Andrzej smiled. "What did you say?"

"I told him of our conditions. I pleaded with him to find a way to release us."

"And? How did he get the letter?" He was mocking his wife.

"I gave the letter to the man who gave me the meagre food portions each day." She paused. "I told him to go the train station and throw the letter onto the train to Moscow."

"And just like that, he followed your orders?" He continued his mocking approach.

"I bribed him."

"With what?"

"My brassiere."

"You gave this man your brassiere?" He laughed.

"Yes! I was desperate! I had to do something to rescue my family, the other families!"

"And what makes you think Stalin even received this letter?"

She was silent as he glanced back at the rough road that led them further and further away from the rusted portals of Siberia.

Andrzej smiled again at his wife, and he put his hand in hers. Their footsteps matched each other's as the bitter wind whipped around their ankles.

* * *

Ewa held her sister's hand. It was warm in hers. Most of the time, Agnieszka wanted to be picked up and carried. She was so little, so scared of life. Their parents, but mostly Agata, tried to reassure them both that this was all an adventure, and everything would work out fine. Ewa was taught to not express fear, but somehow her little sister was able to by-pass this notion and cried often. Above all, her little sister avoided their parents and ran to Agata who would hold her and comfort her.

That day, as Agata walked alongside the children, mindful of the sisters who were holding hands, something that rarely happened, she was quiet. Everyone seemed deep in thought as they all slowly moved forward on a path that would begin the next phase of their lives.

The exuberance of the early morning had transformed into a drudging of each step as the cold and their collective exhaustion took over. By the end of the afternoon, still no one talked as each member of that family stared at their feet. Agnieszka dreamed of sidewalks bathed in sunlight. Ewa thought of a new pair of shoes, as she looked at the holes in the ones she was wearing. Gosia tried to ignore the hunger pains that rumbled inside her, as she dreaded the worst possible outcome for her family. Andrzej's brain rumbled incessantly around logarithms he had memorized in his early days as a student in the University. Agata thought of her son, missing him, wondering where he was if he was still alive.

They reached the train station. On one of the pillars was a large sign that read *"Station Closed indefinitely."*

"We will need to walk to the next station." Andrzej looked at his wife.

"How far is that?"

"About two hours by foot."

Gosia was silent. She had developed blisters on her feet.

* * *

They had no food to eat, the night had fallen, and freedom seemed like an illusion. They were all alone, and the silence of the tundra slammed into their ears.

"I hear horse hooves!" Agata announced.

Everyone looked up. There was nothing visible in front of or behind them. They all stopped walking and listened.

"I hear horse hooves too!" Ewa stated.

"Nonsense!" Andrzej said. "It's your imagination. There is no one here! We must walk. We must leave the Gulag!"

"I am not walking anymore! Enough is enough!" Gosia stared at the empty road.

"Maybe Stalin has a chariot for us?" Andrzej laughed.

"It's not funny. I think I hear horses too."

"So now my whole family has gone mad?"

"Shh…" Agnieszka looked at her father and frowned.

The snow became heavier. Thick freezing flakes surrounded them and covered the road. Agnieszka began to shiver. Agata picked her up and held her close.

"We must move on. We cannot stand here any longer. We will get covered by this snow."

"We will not move on. We will all die here on Russian soil if we must." Gosia glared at her husband.

Before Andrzej could say anything in response, Ewa screamed out: "They are here!"

Fifty meters behind them were two horses pulling a covered carriage.

Andrzej, flushed with energy, moved to the center of the road, and waved his arms wildly. The horses came to an abrupt halt. A burly man got out of the carriage. He wore a thick fur coat.

"Please, sir, my family needs help."

"I can't help you." He grumbled. He motioned to a baby in the back seat of the carriage. "My wife just died. I am taking the baby to live with her grandmother."

"I am so very sorry for your loss, sir. So very sorry."

"I don't need your sympathy. Just get out of my way. The horses can't move while you are standing here. If you don't move, I will have them trample you and your family."

"We have a 5-ruble gold coin." Gosia looked the man in the eyes.

The man averted his eyes away from Gosia.

"Where are you going?"

"The closest train station."

"They just closed all the stations. Too many passengers and they couldn't manage it. So, they closed everything."

"So, Samarkand then?" Andrzej looked at the man with a firm gaze.

"Are you crazy? That's 3000 kilometers!"

"Yes, I know." Andrzej now stared at the man with pleading eyes.

"I can take you to Krasnoyarsk. From there you can hop a train. I have heard they haven't closed the station there yet. Surely no one will notice a man and four females." He smirked. "Get on quickly before I change my mind." He held out his hand. Gosia reached into her pocket and pulled out the coin and gave it to Andrzej. He placed it in the man's hand. He nodded, then helped the girls and the women into his carriage. He motioned for Agata to hold the baby in her lap. Everyone was squished together, and the horses began to move.

There was a fresh loaf of bread in a white paper on the floor. The man noticed Ewa's eyes staring at it.

"Hungry?"

She nodded.

"Take as much as you want and share some with your little sister." Ewa tore off a piece for Agnieszka and one for herself. They ate ravenously. The man smiled. Then he looked sad. He glanced at his baby, and then looked down at his feet. He had tears in his eyes.

"Hard times." Agata saw the man's tears. She looked at the baby in her lap and stroked his soft cheeks, warm from sleep.

The man nodded. It seemed like he wanted to look at Agata and the baby, but he kept his gaze on the road, at the last rays of light before the falling of the night.

* * *

It was midday the next day when they arrived at the train station in Krasnoyarsk. It was snowing hard. Andrzej shook the man's hand, Gosia thanked him, and they all watched him get back in the carriage and direct the horses to continue his path.

Hundreds of people lined the station, waiting for the train that was already eight hours late.

"Excuse me, sir?" Andrzej asked one of the people who was on the platform. "Where is this train coming from?"

"Tavda." The passenger grunted.

"But there is no station in Tavda."

"There is now. Just opened a week ago. So many passengers heading to Samarkand, sir."

Andrzej nodded and scowled at the ground. He walked over to his wife.

"That scoundrel!"

"What scoundrel?"

"The man who took our gold."

"What about him?"

"I should have known better."

"What happened?"

"He got us completely out of the way!"

"What do you mean?"

"A week ago, a train station opened in Tavda."

"But maybe he didn't know?"

"Of course, he knew. As soon as you produced gold, he jumped at the chance to play a trick on us and took us as far east as he could in the middle of the night. To think we were only an hour or less from the train station." He paused.

"He was looking at Agata and played on her kindness. He wanted someone to hold his baby that he was going to get rid of. I bet he couldn't bear to hold the infant and wanted Agata to take care of her all the way to his parents' house in Krasnoyarsk."

"So now we have to retrace our steps?"

"Not exactly. We must go southwest instead of directly south. A difference of about twenty-four hours."

Gosia sighed. She reached out and held her husband's hand, feeling the sweat pouring out.

"*His hand never sweats*," she thought. She looked up at his face, noticing the fatigue that lined his thick eyebrows.

* * *

The station was a battered building that looked like it had been bombed a few hours earlier. There was no station agent. There was no way to try to purchase a ticket. Andrzej went searching for someone who might know how to help his family. Gosia paced the platform, looking up at the hundreds of people who were also trying to get on that train.

"The man said we would be hopping the train. How do we do that, Agata?" Agnieszka looked up at the sweet face of the woman she trusted and loved more than anyone else in the world.

"Well, my darling, when the train comes, you will just have to hold on tight to my hand, and when I say jump, you must jump up onto the train."

"But there are so many people who will be doing the same thing. What if there is no space for all of us? Or what if we miss and fall on the tracks?" Ewa asked, reading her sister's mind.

"You absolutely will not fall on the tracks, and of course there will be space for all our family."

"There will be space for everyone here at the station?"

"That I don't know, my love. I hope that everyone who wants to get on that train will get on that train."

"What if the train doesn't come? And what if it does come, but it doesn't stop?"

"It will come. And it will stop, my sweet."

Agnieszka and Ewa were quiet and pensive after that, gazing down at the length of the tracks. Snow fell on their noses, and they didn't seem to care. Ewa was looking at the tracks, following the smooth line of metal and ice. Then she walked over to her father and tightly held his hand. Agnieszka cuddled up close to Agata and stayed there, attached to her like a cat.

* * *

A few hours later, the sound of the train rumbled and echoed off the snowy tundra. The hundreds of passengers at the station started to scream as they got ready to jump on the train upon its arrival.

Pandemonium filled the air as the huge, black and sooty locomotive slowly appeared around the bend. It gradually came to a complete stop as people ran wildly and started to leap onto it. The train conductor was old and looked tired, as he attempted to blow a whistle, but not much sound came out. He shook his head as he witnessed the hundreds of people at the station risking their lives to get on. His expression was one of resignation as he limped back onto the train trying to find a place to stand amidst the hordes that seemed ready to crush him.

Ewa didn't look around at the masses of people that surrounded her. She looked at her father, who nodded, signaling that it was time to jump. Her brain wasn't engaged as her feet leapt from the platform onto the train. Then she held on tight to a railing as she looked down. Agata held her sister and then threw her in the air, up to Ewa who caught her. Agata jumped, landed gracefully on the train and then held the two children close to her. Then, she motioned for Ewa to hold tight onto her sister as Andrzej lifted his wife and handed her into Agata's waiting, strong arms. The four of them held onto each other firmly as the train started to slowly move from the station. Hundreds of people were screaming to get on, and those who were on were screaming for their loved ones who didn't make it.

Gosia, Agata, Ewa and Agnieszka all screamed out, "*Tatuś, Kochanie, Andrzej!*"

Andrzej clutched solidly to the family's only suitcase as he ran after the train which was gathering speed out of the station. He ran faster than he had ever run in his life. He looked up and spotted his wife, screaming at him as the train edged out of the station, while the screams and wails of hundreds of people blanketed the world around him. He ran to the very end of the paved part of the station, he quickly looked up at his wife again and then, without thinking, he threw the suitcase where she was standing and then he threw his entire body up in the air like a balloon and thumped at her feet. He grabbed onto her ankles as his eyes teared up, as his wife sighed, as his children knelt and hugged him and Agata smiled.

* * *

They traveled for almost two weeks by train.

There was nowhere to sit, nowhere to sleep, nowhere to even go to the bathroom. The toilets were clogged. There was no food to eat. Everyone's bodies were covered with lice.

Once, Andrzej left for a few hours. He returned carrying a loaf of bread.

"Where did you get this?" Gosia asked.

He winked.

"Do you remember Dr. Abend?"

"Is he on the train?" Gosia thought of the physician she had seen that one time in the camp when she was so ill. Her husband's parents had met his parents in Krakow so many years ago. He had told her that he would be transferred to Samarkand the next week, and if ever her family had a need for help, he would be there.

"No, but his old neighbor is. Alexander." He paused. "Nice fellow. He was recently released from a deportation camp for single persons."

"And he gave you that bread? How did he get it?"

"Somehow, he has connections. Don't ask me how." He smiled.

Gosia shook her head. She looked at her husband with incredulousness. She tore at the bread ravenously and stuffed a piece in her mouth. She gave the rest to Agata who broke it into pieces for the children, saving a tiny bit for herself. Everyone ate like wild animals, biting into the hard crust of the bread with teeth that could kill. Passengers around them yelled and tried to snatch the bread, but Andrzej glared at them. Agnieszka, seeing the vicious hands that tried to grab her food, began to cry and accidentally dropped her piece on the ground. The starving passengers, like vultures, swooped down and grabbed the last piece of bread, leaving her with nothing.

In those two weeks they had to change trains every few days and wait for hours at stations. No one ever knew when the next train would come. Each time they had to get on the next train, there was pandemonium, screaming and crying. Hundreds of passengers would be left at stations because there was no room. Train conductors screamed orders that no one heard above all the noise, so they took their bully sticks and whipped any passenger who tried to get on the train when it was about to move.

The stench was overwhelming. The windows wouldn't open to let in any air, and feces seeped out all over the passenger cabins. At night, all the passengers had to sleep packed together on the floor, and hordes of lice crawled from one person to another.

In the middle of October 1942, they arrived in Samarkand, the second largest city in Uzbekistan. When the war had broken out, the Uzbeks hoped that Hitler would liberate them from the Russians, and they had prepared a big flag with a swastika to be hung in the city hall.

Agnieszka, held in Agata's arms, looked back at the crowd of endless bodies pushing each other out of the station. Ewa held her father's hand, and Gosia stood weakly at her husband's side as they stepped forth into the next stage of their lives. It was exceptionally cold, and light snow fell around them.

The N.K.V.D., the People's Commissariat for Internal Affairs, the Soviet secret police agency screamed out orders, directing the Poles away from the train station. They wanted the refugees to get out of the way. Anyone who had not found their own lodgings by nightfall would be chased onto rail trucks and sent to the countryside to pick cotton.

Andrzej looked around him at the chaos. Amid the crowd, he spotted Alexander. He approached him and smiled.

Reading his mind, he whispered in Andrzej's ear, "You can stay in my room with me."

Andrzej looked at him, incredulously. "All five of us?"

"Yes, follow me."

They went up and down the side streets, through narrow alleyways. It was dark and the snow was getting heavier when they arrived at a shabby brown door. Alexander pulled out a key from his pocket. There was one room, one bed and a sink and toilet.

"How did you know about this place?"

"My neighbor gave me the key." He paused. "He owns this apartment, but he does not stay here. He has another place across town."

"Dr. Abend?"

"Yes."

Andrzej nodded. He smiled weakly. He put his hand to his head, rubbing it. His legs trembled. For a moment it looked like he was unable to stand.

No one noticed. The children ran around the room like marmosets in a jungle.

Agata pulled each child to the floor and began the long process of getting out the lice that had infested everyone's hair.

The next day, Alexander left, and found a job across the street as a janitor for the military hospital. That night, he smuggled into the apartment raisins, almonds, and chocolate for the children. Ewa and Agnieszka squealed with delight as they devoured the delicacies, hugging Alexander, and dancing around him. They were all singing; this was the first time anyone had sung for months.

That night, when the children were asleep, and Alexander had gone back to work to do the night shift, Andrzej could barely pull off his shirt when he was getting ready for bed. There were spots all over his body. Suddenly, he became unconscious, and he began to hallucinate. Gosia put her hand on his forehead. He was burning with fever.

She paced back and forth in the room, staring at him, not knowing what to do, worrying, and crying. *He can't die. He can't die,* she whispered to herself.

He muttered something incoherent, and then he stopped, and his eyes turned back in his head.

Oh my God, is he dead?

She paced more furiously than before. Her children and Agata were snoring on the other side of the room.

She stared at his chest. There was a rise and fall.

He's not dead! Thank God!

He opened his mouth to say something. All that came out were jumbled words. His eyes were shut. Then he sat up and opened his eyes. They were red and inflamed.

"Dr. Abend!" he mouthed. Then he lay down and convulsed. His body writhed and his fever shot up.

Gosia paced more frantically. She went to the door, opened it, and shut it.

Where is he…Dr. Abend? Where is he?

Just then, Alexander walked in. It was three in the morning, and he had just gotten off his night shift. He took one look at Andrzej and shook his head.

"Typhus, Madam. We must get him out of here, otherwise you and the children will surely get it."

"We need to find Dr. Abend! My husband needs him!"

"He is not in Samarkand now, Madam. He is stationed in Kermine and is unable to leave until Friday. He comes back home sometimes on Friday nights and returns on Sunday morning." He paused. "That's if they allow him to leave Kermine for the weekend." I will take him to the hospital across the street. At least he will be away from the family. There are doctors there." He looked away.

"This is serious. He needs Dr. Abend."

"I will do what I can Madam."

He wrote down something on a piece of paper.

"This is his address. It's on the nice side of town. Maybe you can go there and wait for him on Friday evening. Perhaps he will be there. I will do what I can to see if he can come this week. Meanwhile, I will try to get a doctor to see your husband." He paused and looked down.

"I am only a janitor."

Gosia looked at him with desperation.

He nodded and then went over to Andrzej and roused him. He propped him up and supported him, encouraging him to walk. Andrzej was mostly limp.

"Damn it. We need a stretcher!" he muttered to himself.

"You must try to walk, Andrzej. We must get you across the road to the hospital."

"Dr. Abend!" Andrzej mouthed; his voice was barely audible. Extremely weak, his face haggard, he looked at his wife with a resigned yet pleading look.

"Don't talk. Save your energy for the walk."

Alexander used all his strength to hold Andrzej up. He was sweating as he had his arm around him and propelled him out the door, down the stairs, and outside.

It was snowing hard, and the ground was mostly frozen.

Andrzej was sweating and shivering, and his fever soared as he stumbled and fell, sliding on the ice.

Gosia stood at the window, watching it all, as she paced with frenzy.

Don't die. Don't die. Don't die, she begged as the snow fell harder and harder outside. She watched Alexander pick up her husband and carry him around his shoulders as they crossed the street. Never had she seen him so ill. He was the rock of her life.

She felt her heart beating rapidly, as she held firmly to the piece of paper with the address of Dr. Abend.

* * *

The next day Gosia went to the hospital and pleaded with the nurses to at least give her husband a proper hospital bed in a proper hospital room. He was delirious and burning with fever on a stiff gurney in the hallway. He did not even recognize his wife.

"Not only should you not be here, Madam, as he is highly contagious, but you need to know we are doing the best we can. Go home, please. Your husband has a confirmed case of typhus. We are doing everything we can do within our medical and space restraints."

The nurse gave Gosia a reluctant, hasty look, and then scurried down the hall.

Gosia did not move, did not leave her husband.

The same nurse returned an hour later.

"Madam, if you don't leave this hospital at once, I will have to call the hospital attendants to forcibly remove you."

"But when will the doctor see my husband?"

"There is one doctor for hundreds of patients. He will see your husband when it's his turn to be seen. The doctor comes once a week. That is all the information I have to give you. The nurses are attending to your husband. Now leave at once. I will see you to the door."

She pointed to the door, motioning for her to get out. Gosia walked reluctantly. The nurse did not leave her sight until she was outside.

Then she locked the door.

Gosia headed for home. It was snowing and hard flakes of ice hit her nose. No one was home when she returned. Agata had taken Agnieszka out. Ewa was also away. She was accustomed to walking the narrow streets and littered alleys of the old city to the bazaar, where she sold all her mother's clothes, her father's shoes, and anything else she could find. She spoke Russian fluently and bargained her wares for a few rubles. Other days, she would walk two to three miles to the newer part of town carrying baskets full of empty bottles she had collected from peoples' backyards, earning a few kopeks for them. She exchanged this money for hard candies she would bring home to provide sweeteners for tea.

Gosia paced in the empty apartment. The quiet surrounded her. She spent the entire morning mumbling to herself. *Let him not die. Let him not die.*

Each day she would return to the hospital, hoping that the nurse who kicked her out was not there. For two days she was, and upon seeing Gosia she looked at her with threatening eyes and forbade her from entering the building.

On the third day she was gone, and Gosia ventured quietly inside. She did not see her husband in the hallway. She inquired at the front desk about his whereabouts.

"We are very busy, Madam. Come back tomorrow." the receptionist said coldly.

"Is he here in this hospital?"

"Yes. He's here. He was transferred to another wing, and I will have the information for you tomorrow."

Gosia left the building again, this time walking up and down the streets, with her mind focused on only one thing.

To distract herself, she went to the small center run by a Polish refugee committee. They distributed milk and bread for families with children. That day, someone had put up a poster with an announcement.

"All Polish subjects, except Polish Byelorussians, Polish Ukrainians, and Jews, may report for military service. Meet at the town square at 8 a.m. on October 26, 1942."

She went to the desk at the center and approached a Polish colonel who was working there.

"Excuse me, Sir, but can you please tell me why Jews are excluded from military service? We have always been loyal and trustworthy citizens."

"It is not up to us, Madam. This is the order of the N.K.V.D." He took one look at her, walked away and pretended to busy himself with a project with one of the volunteers.

Disgusted, she went back out into the street and kept walking. She pulled out the piece of paper that Alexander had given her and memorized the address.

As she walked, she recalled the day she had met Dr. Abend. He had come to Siberia for a few months to fill in for a doctor who was having a baby. She was granted permission to see him once because she was losing weight and running a fever. He had given her a two week's leave of absence which the camp commandant had torn up when she had shown it to him. On that occasion, Dr. Abend had told her his story. She was at first struck by the fact that he had come from Nowy Sacz, a small town in Poland where her maternal ancestors were born. He had said he had heard of her great-great grandfather, who was a well-known rabbi. He had told her he had lost his entire family to the Germans a few years earlier.

"I will never forgive myself," he had said as the rain fell silently outside.

"In September 1939 the Polish government ordered me to do a special assignment treating patients away from home in Bialystok. The doctor there had fallen in a snow accident, and had broken his leg, and there were no other doctors in town. I told them I couldn't do it, that my family was in Warsaw, and I couldn't leave them.

'Nonsense!' they told me. 'You do as you are instructed.'

'Can I bring my family there?'

'Absolutely not. This is not a resort hotel.' Then the officer walked away.

"Did they know I was Jewish? Did they not know that Hitler was advancing in the west and that Warsaw was next to be taken over? Why did I even listen to him? Why didn't I smuggle my wife and children to safety? I was such a fool! Such an awful fool!"

He had gone silent and cried.

"I wrote to them but got no answer. I wrote to our neighbors then. I waited for a month, and finally I got a telegram from them. The day after I left, in the middle of the night, there was a hard knock on the door, and there was a truck waiting outside, and they shoved my beautiful wife and my two children into that truck. No one has seen them since."

Dr. Abend wept. Then he stopped and looked at the ground.

"You will meet my husband. We will be friends." Gosia said in a quiet voice.

Bronek Abend looked up and nodded.

* * *

She didn't know this side of town, and she quickly got lost. She roamed and roamed the streets of Samarkand. Hunger filled her belly. She hadn't eaten since the day before, but she did not pay attention to

66

the rumblings that persisted. She ended up on Street of the Muses. At number 68, there was a Mezuzah on the door frame. She almost fainted, seeing it. She quietly knocked. No one answered. She turned the door handle and without hesitation, it opened. She gasped and walked in.

There, bathed in candlelight, was Dr. Abend. He was in prayer, reciting the mourner's *kaddish* as the *yahrzeit* candle burned by his side. Everything seemed to stand still as generations of the dead were soothed, held, and blessed.

* * *

Andrzej vacillated between states of consciousness. Never had he been this ill.

I am dying.

His fever soared to numbers even the thermometer could not read. His body convulsed and when he wasn't vomiting, he could only lie on the hard piece of board that was his bed. The doctor had still not seen him. His moans accompanied hundreds of others around him. The smells of urine, vomit, and defecation swirled around his nostrils.

Where am I?

He tried to get up, but the weakness and achiness in his legs prevented him from moving. He fell to the floor and lay there, sprawled out like a corpse.

His was a life of immutability. He had learned at an early age that sternness and resilience were what life was about. While he had a deep-seated softness for his wife and his children, he maintained a calm and steadfast iron-clad strength in everything he encountered in the world. He was brilliant, resourceful and, in his work as an engineer, there was nothing he couldn't master and resolve.

Dying was never a thought he entertained. That was for the other breed, the one that succumbed to weakness.

He returned to an unconscious state, there on the floor in the middle of a hospital in Samarkand. His leg twisted, and possibly broken, in that moment he did not even know that he was gravely ill, and in fact, just hours away from death.

* * *

Night had fallen. Agnieska was asleep in Agata's arms.

"Where is *Matka*, and where is *Tatuś*?" Ewa looked in the eyes of her nanny.

"Your *Tatuś* is a little sick, and your *Matka* is with him in the hospital." She smoothed out Ewa's greasy hair. "They will be back soon."

Agata had taught the children not to worry, not to question further, to believe that what she told them was infinitely true. She was extremely skilled in hiding her own worried thoughts.

"Now, let's count how many pebbles we collected today."

Agata began to quietly sing an old Polish drinking song, its bawdy and reckless lyrics she muffled, as her melodious voice sweetly rang out. Ewa smiled.

"One, two, three, four, five, six, seven, eight."

"Look, Aga, I found eight!"

"Lovely! There's more in my pockets. There are some beautiful pebbles here in Samarkand."

Agata had mastered the art of distraction, but she also knew that this method completely worked with the two girls. Her devotion to them was unstoppable as was her fervent optimism, in the face of everything.

She had never told the girls about her son. When she had accepted the position as a nanny for Gosia and Andrzej, she had thought it would be temporary, and she had begged her mother to watch over her own child who was three years old at the time. She had needed the money to support her son and parents. Her father, blinded by a mine accident, was unable to work. Her mother gave up her job as a secretary at the mine to care for her grandson, who had severe epilepsy. When Gosia and Andrzej had to escape western Poland, they had begged Agata to stay with them. Agata had become quite attached to Ewa, and she agreed. She had regularly secretly written to her family, sending them monthly checks, but she had never seen her son again since she left him when he was three.

At the beginning of the war, Gosia had asked her why she would abandon her son, leave Poland, and come with them. Agata had replied: "These are my children." She had pointed to Ewa and Agnieszka. In that moment, it seemed there was another reason she was hiding. Her eyes turned downward and focused on the ground. She had never revealed the real reason. Instead of returning to her home village and family, she spent those eight years risking her life and experiencing the hardships, chaos, and uncertainty of life as a prisoner and refugee.

* * *

"Dr. Abend!" Gosia stifled her scream. No one was to know she was there.

He opened his eyes and looked up from his prayer.

"*Pani Majewski!*" His sunken eyes radiated light.

"You must help me quickly. My dear husband asked for you. He is dying. They say it is typhus!"

"Oh my god!"

"Can you help him? Quickly?"

"Yes. Of course. I will try." He paused. "The best medicine is not available." He stopped again and fingered his beard. "But I have a way to obtain some. I will have to bribe the pharmacy to get me a vial."

His face darkened "I have no money, *Pani.* The Russians have taken everything I had." He paused. "What they didn't confiscate in Kermine, they stole one night when I was sleeping."

"Oh my God! I am so sorry." She stared at the yahrzeit candle. There was no time for staring, though.

"I have two gold ingots in my suitcase, hidden."

He nodded. "That should be enough. They might need to have them converted to rials, but I think gold speaks louder than rials these days. I can't be seen accompanying you to your apartment. Can you get those ingots, and bring them right back here? Say, in a few hours? It will still be dark."

"Thank God, Doctor, you are a miracle worker!"

"I don't know. I will do what I can. Your husband is a great man." He paused. "Now go quickly and be safe."

Gosia ran swiftly through the streets of Samarkand. Normally, she hated running and would have noticed that she hadn't eaten for what seemed like days. Normally, she would have been teaching at the University, a class of adoring students hanging onto each of her words.

But there was no normal anymore.

She remained conscious of anyone following her, but strangely, the streets at that hour were completely empty. She arrived at the apartment and vaguely listened to the sleeping sounds of Agata and the children who were nestled next to her.

She opened her suitcase and found the small, well concealed zipper that revealed the double-bottomed, hidden section of the case. She took out the envelope and held it to her chest, listening to the soft chinks of metal. She slipped the envelope into her underwear and began to run.

A cold rain hit her, soaking her hair, her dress, and her shoes as she approached the Street of the Muses. She was completely out of breath as she tried the door. It was locked this time.

Where is he? This can't be! She felt desperation encompass her as she tried the door again.

This can't be!

She never prayed, except during the High Holidays when it was expected.

God, please help! Please let my dear husband live! Please let Dr. Abend arrive and please let him get the medicine so that he can live. Please God!

She knew not to stay in one place and wait. She walked a bit down the street. It was still dark, but she knew light would be arriving soon, and she would have to hurry home.

He will arrive. He will arrive. He will arrive.

She walked back to his apartment, then down another side street and back. She walked down yet another side street and then retraced her steps.

From a distance, someone was coming. It was a man about the size of Dr. Abend, short and thin. She hid behind a building and waited; her heart was beating fast. As the man approached, she sighed and reached into her underwear to pull out the envelope.

Dr. Abend greeted her with a hurried smile as she handed him the envelope.

"I have the medicine." he whispered as he tucked the envelope in his jacket pocket.

Gosia wept quietly and sighed.

"Go now, it will be light soon. I will be at the hospital in one hour. I will find your husband and give him the medicine. He will live, Gosia. He will live."

Chapter Thirteen

My two sisters and I all have "baby books": thick albums that recount our lives from birth to young adulthood. They are my mother's most treasured possessions. I have always thought that if there was a fire, the baby books would be the only things she would save. Not only was she meticulous in recording the minutest details of our developmental milestones, but more importantly, she poured an infinite amount of love and devotion into each of these books. There are pages and pages of descriptions of things we have done. And, at the end of the book, there are pages and pages of photos my father and grandfather took of my sisters and me that she painstakingly arranged with those sticky corners that she affixed to each page. She then annotated each photo.

Although I never witnessed her working on these books, I imagine she must have spent countless hours on their creation. When did she find the time to do this? Perhaps in the wee hours of the night, when her husband was snoring, her children were deep in their own slumbers, when she could not or did not want to sleep, she stayed awake and thought about her children as she wrote and felt happy to be a mother. She told us often that being a mother was the happiest thing in her life.

Nowhere do I sense trauma in the creation of these books, in her thoughts of being a mother, in her post-wartime existence. Rather, she seemed to live in a state of extended joy, living vicariously through her children, their adorableness, their accomplishments, and their very existence, perhaps. Her favorite pictures are the ones where the three of us sisters show love and devotion to each other, something which did not happen very often. We, like most sisters, squabbled quite a bit. We were somewhat like cats, fighting over territory. I was resented by my sisters because I was the youngest and I took up valuable physical and psychological space from my mother. But my mother never focused on this fact. She seemed to live in such a blissful existence where all was well with the world of her and her children. She had a husband, parents and steady clients from her psychotherapy practice, but at the base of everything that made her happy was her daughters. I often wonder if she either had an uncanny ability to repress anything painful, or if she allowed her unconscious to deny anything that had hurt her. Or both.

Which is precisely why it is so interesting that she passed on such an intense level of trauma, when she herself was not experiencing any of it. Or at least, consciously.

She told me once that she had gone to a psychoanalyst, a Dr. D, because, as she said to me, "She thought she should." Then, she added, "Rose (her best friend) told me it might be a good idea given my past."

I was too young to understand what she meant. Besides, we were brought up to never ask personal questions of our parents.

She told me that Dr. D had told her that of all his clients, she was the one who was most in denial of her feelings. I don't know why she told me this. I discovered she hadn't told my sisters when I asked them, years later. I remember she kind of smirked when she related to me what her therapist had told her, as if she oversaw the magnificent job her unconscious was doing, as if she attached herself to the idea that she was perhaps his favored client in denial.

I think she never left this unconscious bubble she had surrounded herself with. I know she went to see him a few times a week for many years. Maybe she did relay the stories of her past, but with no feeling attached. Maybe she never told her stories at all or alluded to them once in the beginning when he asked about her past. I will never know. My mother is such a mysterious vault.

Except when it came to her daughters. I know, with complete certainty, that we must have rescued her from experiencing any past trauma that might have surfaced in her American life. Just our being on this planet, documented in those thick pages of our baby books, was a testament to her devotion to motherhood, to the power she gave us to transcend the ugliness of the world.

Chapter Fourteen

Andrzej, healed from the typhus, got a job with the city of Samarkand's building department. His first job was to build a shelter for incoming refugees. He oversaw men and women who had arrived from labor prisons and his instructions were to build fences and a watchtower so they could not escape. Communist party officials demanded that bricks be used for the foundation, but despite many attempts, Andrzej could not acquire any bricks for the project. He was threatened by the same officials that he would be guilty of sabotage if he did not somehow obtain those bricks. At the same time, he was given an assignment to build a courtyard for a party official in town. This project required bricks. The materials arrived that same day. Somehow the bricks were available for officials, but not refugees.

Meanwhile, because of the agreement that Stalin had made with Polish General Sikorski, a Polish army was being formed in the Soviet Union to go to Great Britain to join the Allied forces. Their families would be sent to East Africa, which was then under British rule, for asylum during the war. Any able-bodied man was accepted, except those who admitted to being Jewish. In the late fall of 1942 Andrzej applied, so he could leave Russia once and for all. Officials placed him in Category A, but then, upon interviewing him and finding out he was Jewish, they quickly rescinded his application.

Later that week, Andrzej and Gosia were invited to Dr. Abend's house for an informal gathering. At that party a sergeant in the Polish army was visiting from Kermine whose name was Ignacy Jerzyna. Andrzej and Ignacy took an instant liking to each other as they sipped wine. In low voices they talked about their lives. Andrzej told him about his plight. "We are assuming you are a Polish citizen, and not of Jewish ancestry?" Ignacy asked, in a regular voice, as he winked at Andrzej.

"Of course," he answered, winking back.

Ignacy continued, in a voice barely above a whisper.

"I will list your wife as my sister, and you as my brother-in-law. Your two daughters will be listed as my nieces. You will be Polish Catholics. The next transport will be in August, and it is strictly reserved for army personnel and their families."

Andrzej smiled before he frowned. "We have no money to pay you."

"I am not doing it for money. I only want to help you."

He then took out a piece of paper and wrote down the name of his mother, his father, the church where he was married and the priest who married him and his wife.

"Memorize this. Your wife too." he whispered. "I will notify you when it is time to come to Kermine." Then he walked away, stepped outside and hailed a taxi.

Two weeks later, Andrzej received a telegram.

"You and your family are expected in Kermine tomorrow by noon. Report to the Polish army headquarters, four hundred meters south of the train station."

That afternoon, Andrzej went to the train station to buy train tickets for him and his family. There were none. The trains were always crowded with refugees. Everyone wanted to escape.

Determined to leave Russia, Andrzej went in silently into the officers' quarters that night after everyone had left. He had never stolen anything in his life and his palms were sweating profusely as he quietly took six bottles of expensive vodka from the cabinet that was reserved for visiting Communist officials, to impress them when they came to Samarkand. He put the bottles in his suitcase, and quickly made his way home.

Without a word, he opened his suitcase and showed his wife what he had. She gasped.

"Passage to Kermine," was all he said as he got into bed with his clothes still on.

"When do we leave?" Gosia whispered in his ear. She pressed her body against him.

"Tomorrow at 6 a.m."

She listened to him snore as she lay awake all night.

* * *

Early the next morning Andrzej and his family stood at the train station in Samarkand. The sun was rising, and the early morning smells of summer wafted around them. Although he was technically healed from the typhus, Andrzej still felt weak and had little appetite. He had lost so much weight during that two-week episode.

He hardly recognized his family, let alone himself, with their newly shaven heads that bobbed like air bubbles in a pond. The new clothes they were given to prevent the spread of lice also seemed strange and did not resemble at all what they had on when they arrived, clothes that were immediately burned. The station was terribly overcrowded, and babies were crying. Everyone at the station looked tired, forlorn, and overwhelmed.

He had just one suitcase, which was mostly filled with bottles of vodka.

At the station, Agata distracted the children while Gosia paced along the platform.

Andrzej walked over to the station agent and motioned for him to let him into the office. He opened his suitcase, producing the liquor. Trying his best to show confidence, he announced "passage for me and my family, please." The station agent picked up a bottle and examined it, inspecting the label. He then took all six bottles and put them in a locked cabinet. He nodded, opening a drawer and produced a stack of tickets from Samarkand to Kermine. He handed these to Andrzej.

Five minutes later, the train arrived. Hundreds of people crammed into the open doors, trying to push themselves onto the train. The conductors screamed for everyone to get off except for ticketed passengers while beating with a stick and pushing to the ground anyone who did not have a ticket. An hour passed before the chaos subsided and the train would depart. Andrzej clutched onto their tickets in one hand and his oldest daughter's in the other. His wife was next to him. Agata held the baby in her arms, holding onto the backs of seats so they wouldn't fall. There were no available seats to sit upon, but they were on the train as it slowly moved away from the station.

Once on the train, Gosia sighed quietly and stared out the window. She was still too anxious to say anything to her children, thinking about the stolen bottles of vodka. Agata held Agnieszka and told stories to the two little girls.

Two hours later, they arrived in Kermine.

Agata looked at Ewa as they left the train and walked down the platform, following Andrzej.

"Now, Ewa, if anyone asks you where you are going, why you are here in Kermine, you are to tell them that you are visiting your Uncle Jerzyna." Ewa nodded.

Ten minutes later, a Russian officer stopped the family, turned to Ewa and said, "Hello young lady. I see you are with your family and have just got off the train. Can you please tell me why you are here in Kermine?"

Ewa looked the officer in the eye and with a show of confidence, told him "We are visiting my Uncle Jerzyna."

"Thank you. Have a nice visit." Then he walked away.

* * *

They made their way to the Polish army headquarters, along with hundreds of others. Officers directed families to enter a large space with dark walls and peeling paint. Suddenly, a Polish officer rushed into the room and screamed out: "Andrzej Majewski? Is there an Andrzej Majewski in the room?"

His voice was so loud that everyone looked up and stared.

The officer sternly said to Gosia: "Please leave the station at once with your children. Andrzej, follow me!"

The soldier led Andrzej to the police station.

"What is your true name, sir?" The officer's voice was harsh and cold.

"Andrzej Majewski."

"You are lying. If you don't tell me your true identity there will be harsh consequences."

"Andrzej Majewski, sir."

"You have been lying. There is punishment for this."

Andrzej was sweating, but his face showed nothing.

"I will release you and your family on the condition that you leave Kermine immediately."

He opened the door and pushed Andrzej out. He tumbled to the ground, brushed off his clothes and went back to the train station to see if he could obtain tickets for travel out of the city. Crowds of people surrounded him, all trying to obtain tickets. The chaos was deafening. Finding tickets was impossible and finding his wife and children was equally challenging. He asked officer after officer where his family might be. Finally, after four hours of investigation, he was pointed in the direction of some dilapidated army barracks. There, amidst babies crying and domestic squabbles, his wife and children sat on the floor, shaking. His daughters were whimpering.

Andrzej said nothing as he held his wife and children close to him.

At 4 a.m., when sleep sounds emanated from the barracks, he silently left the room. Gosia stirred, opened her eyes, and watched him leave. She tensed up, not knowing when or if he would return.

There were two different areas in Kermine. In the middle of the night Andrzej walked the four miles from the village of Kermine to the town. It was very cold, and the wind whipped around his neck. When he reached the town, he walked into the military base. It was early and the sun had not yet risen.

"I would like to speak with the man in charge, a high-ranking officer, please," he asked in perfect Russian. He had woken up the man at the front desk, whose head had collapsed onto the counter. An empty bottle of whiskey lay in a bag on the floor by his feet. There was silence around him, and it appeared that no one was around.

The receptionist stirred and looked up.

"I would like to speak with a high-ranking officer, please?" he repeated.

"But everyone is gone, sir. It's the middle of the night."

"I saw a light in the back. Someone is awake."

The receptionist turned his head, in the direction of the light. He then got up, staggered to the back office and mumbled something to a man who had stripes on his shoulder. The receptionist returned to the desk and ushered Andrzej to the back room.

"Please, sir, I am in need of your assistance." He looked firmly into the eyes of the officer. "I am an engineer and a loyal Polish citizen." He explained his situation.

"This matter is not in my jurisdiction. My comrade can listen to your request. But he is not in yet and you must wait a few hours until he begins work. It's the middle of the night."

Andrzej nodded. He had been reminded many times what time of day it was, and nothing mattered anymore but safe passage for him and his family.

"You may wait at the reception desk until you are called."

Andrzej looked down and counted how many floor tiles were chipped and needed repair. Then he looked up at the ceiling and did the same. Finally, two hours later a young man entered the room and ushered him into the officer's office.

"I was sent by the first officer, sir."

The young officer nodded and looked interested. He was aware that this was not true, but it seemed to get his attention.

Andrzej explained his situation.

"What is your wife's first and maiden name please?"

"Gosia Gross."

The officer was silent and shook his head.

"Is your wife Jewish?"

"Yes."

The officer spoke in French to another official. He asked him what he thought of the matter.

"Sometimes Polish men marry Jewish girls," he responded, in

French. They looked in Andrzej's direction to see if he understood what they were saying. Andrez pretended he did not understand French, even though he was fluent in it.

The young officer nodded. He scanned Andrzej's face, looking for identifiable Jewish features.

He then went to his desk and wrote out an exit permit for Andrzej and his family and gave it his official stamp.

"Exit permit to Iran." Andrzej looked at the four words as he thanked the officer and without expression, silently walked back to the village as the sun began its slow journey to the middle of the sky.

* * *

Pressure was put on Stalin to do something about the overwhelming refugee crisis. He decided to allow some of the Polish military and a very small number of civilians to leave Uzbekistan for Iran; the rest had to remain in Russia.

Those who were allowed to enter Iran were given a ticket to freedom.

The evacuation was by ship from Krasnovodsk to Pahlavi and occurred in two phases. Once they arrived in Iran, almost every refugee was infested with lice, many were ill or dying of disease and there was barely any food to eat. The Polish refugees could not stay long in Iran. Hitler was advancing toward Iran because of his need for oil.

After a few months, many of the Polish refugees were transported elsewhere: to Lebanon, India, Uganda, Rhodesia, Kenya, Tanganyika, South Africa, New Zealand, and Mexico. Those destined for East African countries were put on rickety buses through the mountains to Tehran before being shipped to Africa.

* * *

Gosia was in disbelief when her husband came home later that day. She stared at the little piece of paper that simply stated, "Exit Permit to Iran", four words that opened a free world to her and her family. What she did not know then but would find out afterwards, was that later that day, Polish officials had rounded up every Jewish person and their families and ripped up their exit permits, never allowing them to leave Russian soil. For some reason she never discovered, the officials did not tear up their permits.

That night they boarded the train. Minutes after her family had sat down, Polish military officials started to question passengers, removing many of them from their seats and forcibly pushing them off the train. They approached Andrzej and asked for his papers. They took their time going through each document, for each member of the family, looking up and down each person. Gosia's heart was pounding so fast; she was hoping they wouldn't notice how terrified she was.

The officials handed back the documents to Andrzej, nodded and moved on to the next passengers. It was not until they were clearly out of sight that Gosia allowed herself to breathe.

Eight hours later, they arrived in Krasnovodsk, a seaport on the south side of the Caspian Sea in Soviet Russia. Several hundred Polish families of military men were gathered, recently released from prison and labor camps. Everyone was waiting for the ship to take them to Pahlavi, Iran. Haggard mothers held their emaciated, crying children. Gosia and her family got off the train and stood among them for several hours.

Ewa, who was accustomed to keeping her gaze fixed on the ground, following Agata's instructions throughout the years of this war never to look at the misery around her, suddenly looked up as a mother next to her began to scream. In her arms, her dead infant lay limp. Ewa stared at the child, never having seen someone dead before. The toddler appeared to be the same age as her sister. She vomited. Agata took a handkerchief out of her bag and wiped Ewa's face and her soiled clothes. Then she took her hand and moved her away, across to the other side of her family where she would not be able to see the dead child.

Ewa said nothing. For the rest of her life, she never spoke of this incident. But throughout her life, she would vomit easily in situations that were stressful, but that she could never explain.

Finally, a tiny ship arrived at the port, a vessel that was made for a few dozen people, but would now hold several hundred, transporting them for the three-hour voyage across the Caspian Sea. When the ship docked, everyone ran, pushing each other, screaming, afraid of being left behind. Many people threw their suitcases on the ground, leaving them behind, knowing that there would be no room for them.

Customs officials confiscated all Russian currency, stating that this money was not allowed to be brought into another country.

There was one toilet for hundreds of people, and it was on the lower deck. Everyone had to wait their turn to use it. Parents lifted their children over the railing of the ship so they could urinate into the water. A few times during that long journey, children had slipped from their parents' arms and fallen into the sea, drowning instantly. Mother's screams echoed off the walls of the ship. Shortly after one of those screams, Agnieska tugged at her mother's dress, telling her she had to pee. Andrzej scooped her up and was ready to hold her over the rails.

Gosia yelled: "NO!"

He then took his youngest child in his arms and with one arm around her and the other around a pole, he slid down to the lower deck and from there they waited their turn to go to the toilet. While he was waiting for her to finish, he looked around him and saw that two older people had died on the ship and their corpses were left for the flies and rodents.

Finally, the endless three hours was over, and they sighted land. Gosia sighed and said to herself "*We are finally free.*" Andrzej grasped her hand.

Everyone pushed their way to the front end of the boat. Right before disembarking, each refugee had to have their documents scrutinized once again by Polish officers. The head officer was the same man from Kermine who had kept Andrzej for several hours at the police station and who had ordered him to return to Samarkand. He recognized Andrzej instantly and grabbed his documents, ready to tear them up. He read the four words "Exit Permit to Iran" shook his head and scowled, then looked the other way as Andrzej pushed his family towards the exit of the boat.

* * *

There were nearly 1000 people on that boat that had taken three hours to arrive from Krasnovodsk. They were no longer slaves of Stalin's, even if many of the passengers had died or had become severely ill on that brief voyage. The dead were simply tossed out to sea.

The Persian residents of Pahlavi were given no advance warning that this and the many subsequent boats of Polish refugees would be arriving, Hundreds of people lined up at the port on that early morning to stare, point at and gasp at the numbers of downtrodden filthy, emaciated Europeans, arriving from Russia, who were about to embark onto their soil.

Hours passed before the boat was able to fully unload. Mass pandemonium surrounded everyone on that boat and onshore, as one official screamed to the other. No one knew what to do with all those infested people. A mandatory disinfection procedure would take place immediately after disembarkation, according to Iranian rules.

As the night began to fall, the rain started pouring and as the temperatures quickly dropped to near freezing levels, one by one the refugees were finally allowed off the ship. They were led on foot about a mile away to what was called "Camp Number One", or the "Dirty Camp" where they would sleep on the beach and from there go to disinfection centers. Everyone was ordered to strip off their clothes immediately and officials burned every article of clothing they wore, shaved their heads, fearful of the spread of lice and disease. Camp officials, run by the British Red Cross, distributed clean clothes and fed dates, figs, condensed milk, and canned meat to the emaciated refugees. Only when they were pronounced safe and disease free, they were allowed to proceed to the "Clean Camp," which was called "Camp Number Two".

After ten days, they were allowed to leave, and they boarded a bus that would take them to Tehran.

Agata would not be traveling with them. She had been hired by a Jewish orphanage to help in the transport of children from Samarkand to Iran.

It was very hard for Agnieszka to say goodbye to her, as she waved at her nanny, her life force, from the bus stop. She started to cry and didn't want to get on the bus.

"We'll see her soon," Ewa said to her little sister as she put her arm around her. It was one of the few times that she had shown such warmth and understanding to her sister. Usually that was what Agata did.

As they stood in line to get on the bus, Ewa felt it first, something that was being thrown at them. She winced. Then she looked up and saw hundreds of paper candies and cookies being tossed at them, landing at their feet.

She smiled and picked one up. She looked around her and there, in the center of the station was a group of children no older than herself with baskets of treats that they launched high in the sky, in the direction of the Polish refugees who had landed on their soil for a brief time. The Iranian and the Polish children smiled at each other as the adults seemed oblivious to the candy being thrown into the air.

Ewa and her family boarded the bus. Half an hour later, the vehicle, a rickety machine that looked like it had survived generations of drivers, crammed with far too many passengers, sped through the quiet morning streets of Pahlavi.

* * *

Ewa stared at people's feet, the only vantage point that was accessible, as she stood next to her father and held onto his leg from time to time when the bus seemed to go too fast. She counted the number of brown shoes and black shoes, and she gazed at the thin legs sticking up from them. She had no idea where they were, but she felt like the bus was, in general, going very fast. Had she been able to look out the window, she would have seen that they were on a mountainside, a very steep cliff that hugged the rugged terrain of the Iranian countryside. Had she been up in front of the bus and caught sight of the driver, she would have noticed that he was having problems and, in fact, that the brakes on his bus were failing.

The bus careened down the mountainside and rolled and tumbled through the barren hillside. Barren except for one tree. One solitary Cyprus tree somehow miraculously held the bus in place.

The driver died instantly, from a heart attack. All passengers survived with only minor injuries.

The strongest got out first, through the open windows. One by one, they assisted the other passengers off the bus. Many were crying out of shock, praying aloud that they were miraculously alive.

A truck drove by, with a load of goats in the back. He talked to the passengers and went to the next town, an hour away, to get help.

Eight hours later, another bus arrived that took them all to Tehran.

* * *

Wide, tree-lined avenues and magnificent gardens and groves greeted them, connecting old and new parts of the city. Wealthy beautiful women in European style clothes with silk scarves laced over their heads contrasted the cotton, orange flowered scarves that Polish women were made to wear in the camps. All refugees were placed in temporary camps at the edge of town, a run-down section, owned by the Persian air force that consisted of two large red brick buildings surrounded by a high cement wall. There were cement platforms inside that were used as beds. There were so many of them that many people ended up sleeping on the cement floor or outside. New emigrants were arriving constantly, and around 7000 refugees converged into the small place that eventually became a tent city. Barbed wire fencing surrounded the area. The toilets were primitive and were on the outskirts of the camp, about ten minutes from the barracks. Dysentery and other diseases were rampant.

A few days after Andrzej and his family arrived in Tehran, the news spread that several busloads of orphans were on route from Samarkand. Gosia was thrilled, because Agata would most probably be on one of them. She left the camp and went into town, making her way to the bus station. She had been waiting for more than three hours, when several beaten up buses rolled up. One by one, passengers got off, mostly young and emaciated children under the age of fifteen.

They all looked lost, but still had a bit of hope outlining their brows, a childlike optimism that spread across their faces.

Gosia stared at each one, imagining their plight, feeling their sadness, their loss. One of the children caught her eye as he stepped off one of the buses. She knew him. It was Olek Abend, the only son of their good friend and hero, Dr. Abend. *Had Dr. Abend died?* she wondered.

She approached him. "Olek?" she asked.

"Yes." It appeared he did not recognize Gosia.

"I, and my husband, are good friends of your parents." She paused and did not know what else to say.

As if reading her mind, he answered. "They are not dead."

"Oh, thank God!"

He looked down. There were many things he was not saying.

"I have known about you for many years." She paused. "You are thirteen now?"

"Yes." He looked scared, lost.

"And your father is still in Samarkand?"

"Yes." He looked weary of the questions Gosia kept asking.

"How about if you leave this group and stay with us?"

Olek shifted his weight from one foot to the other.

"We were told to wait here in Tehran for a representative for the Youth Aliyah from Palestine."

"I see." Gosia looked down at the threadbare shoes he was wearing. She then looked at his face and saw his eyes turn away.

"This way, children." Olek walked away and followed the guides who were directing them to their camp. Gosia followed him with her eyes until he disappeared into the crowd. She walked up to someone who looked like he was in charge.

"Excuse me sir, but are there children in this group who are not orphans?"

"Yes, Madam, by permission of the Russian government, there are some children in this transport who are not orphans.

"But where do these children come from? Where are their parents?"

"That, Madam, I am not allowed to disclose. Now, if you please, I have important work to do. Please step out of the way."

Gosia thought how it must have been heart wrenching for Dr. Abend and his wife to label their child an orphan, to put their only son on a ship, not knowing if they would ever see him again. The things parents had to do to allow their children to live in a free country. For years after that moment at the bus stop, she would remember his face, the longing he showed for a new life, the things he did not tell her about what he had left behind.

She continued to look at the other passengers that were exiting the buses. In the last one, a thin woman with dark hair and dark piercing eyes got off. Gosia ran to her and hugged her again and again.

"Agata! Dear sweet Agata!" Gosia could not stop smiling as they talked, walking to the bus that would take them to the run-down camp that was their home.

That night, Gosia began to feel unwell. She was feverish and had chills with intense joint pain. She started vomiting and couldn't stop. She went to the medical facility at the camp. They took one look at her and told her she had malaria. They transported her to a hospital in town, where her fever raged.

* * *

While Gosia was very ill, Andrzej was summoned to the Polish recruiting office. Not caring about his Jewish heritage, army officials had accepted his application for enlistment. All he had to do was wait for the next military transport, and he would leave in a few days to join the Polish army. Later that day, Andrzej visited the agency of the Polish government in exile. While he was there, he saw a friend, Bronek Fryling.

"And how are you doing, Mr. Engineer?" he asked, with a laugh accompanying his warm smile.

Andrzej was about to answer and tell him about his recruitment when a high-ranking officer passed by. "Excuse me sir, are you an engineer?"

"Yes."

"What is your specialty?"

"I am a civil engineer."

"That's splendid! We need civil engineers!"

"For what reason?"

"Polish citizens are being taken to Africa and we need to build and maintain camps for them. This is a prestigious placement. You will always be present in the camp for all necessary repairs and building plans. There will be few men there, as most of our men will be fighting at the front in Europe."

"I am delighted and honored for this, sir, but I am due to report to the army of General Anders in England."

"Oh, it's a small matter. I can give you permission, if you agree to leave tomorrow with the military families."

"My main concern is that my wife is currently in the hospital with a high fever."

"Your wife will then have a nurse and a private railcar compartment. Does that seem manageable?"

"Yes. Perfect. Thank you!"

He scribbled some notes to be given to the doctor at the hospital and handed them to Andrzej. Then he gave him an application to sign. Andrzej carefully signed his name and gave the document to Bronek who stamped it several times.

"Excellent." He gave him the official document.

"This is your contract. It will be renewable every six months. The British government has promised that the refugee camp will remain open to the Polish people until the war is over."

He passed over a pen to Andrzej and motioned for him to sign.

"All the best to you and your family, Andrzej!" He reached out his hand and the two shook hands. Bronek then walked out the door.

The next day, Andrzej and his family were on the train to Ahwaz, the hottest place they had ever been. He was suffering from jaundice, his wife still had malaria, and his youngest daughter had trachoma, a severe eye infection, because of the unbearable heat that brought out swarms of flies. They were housed in warehouses with corrugated metal walls and roofs. The oppressive sun beat down on the metal, so there was never any relief from the heat.

Later that week, they were all on a train to Bandar Shapur, a seaport in southwest Iran, the gateway to the Persian Gulf. From there, they boarded a ship to Karachi, India, across the Persian Gulf and the Arabian Sea. More than four weeks later, they arrived in Karachi. They were housed on grey desert sand, in a camp behind barbed wire. Hyenas and jackals were the only animals around.

Finally, a month after that, the ship was ready to take them to Mombasa and from there to the refugee camp in Tanganyika, where they would live for six years.

There, in the harbor, the ship sat waiting. It was the end of 1942. Thousands of Polish refugees began to board the huge vessel. They had been on two continents. They were disheveled, many without hair, without a home, all of them exhausted. Many of their families had perished from hunger or disease. The ones who remained, the survivors, boarded that ship to Africa, yet another continent that would house them for the duration of the war.

Chapter Fifteen

I wonder how my mother became such a beautiful human being. I envied her. How could she enjoy her children's world, and be so happy when she herself had such a challenging start to life?

I had the opportunity to have children in my early twenties with a partner I was then married to. But I chose not to.

I made this decision because of the depression that lingered. It felt like a spirit that invaded my being, overwhelming me. I could not imagine taking care of another soul. My own self was hard enough.

I hid my depression. I was able to work, finish my graduate degree, have friends and be in a relationship. No one knew of my illness, and it had been ages since I had told my mother about it. I went to a therapist for a few years, and there, I was able to uncover some of it and move through some of the pieces that confounded my life. However, in that therapy I did not make the connection between my condition and my mother's trauma. I guess I still was not ready to look at that part of my family's history.

One year muddled into another while this missing piece was still not resolved and before I knew it, it was too late to have children. Instead, I delved more into my work as a teacher of young children and as a psychotherapist for children and families. I became a consultant, supervisor, and mentor teacher. I traveled extensively, observing early childhood education from a multi-cultural perspective, always developing more paradigms from which to base my understanding of what exactly a young child needs to be contented in their world.

Around every turn in this work, however, there was a nagging sensation that I was missing truly something. For years, I never quite knew what it was. Then, at some point, or maybe all along but I never saw it clearly, I realized that I was spending all my energy trying to understand other people's children, although there was such a gaping hole inside myself from the recognition that I had missed my chance to have one of my own. Even after the therapy I went through, I still had so many private moments where I felt stuck in my existence, a fragility that could not be altered.

Eventually this fragility turned into fibromyalgia.

Fragility weaves through me like rain on a winter's day, a constant presence. I link it to my mother's story which always jars my mind. It's a kind of pain that never seems to be able to be erased. In my family's history, there is a cry, sometimes a scream. It wails in the night reminding me of the maimed world we live in. It is the cry of my ancestors being gassed, being locked up in labor camps behind a barbed wire fence.

In 2004, ten years before I was hit with fibromyalgia, I lived in Paris. That year there was a massive commemoration honoring the sixtieth anniversary of the liberation of Auschwitz. The Hotel de Ville had more than a hundred live interviews of survivors. Using headphones the city provided, I listened to the harrowing voices of old people telling their stories. Their traumas haunted me for weeks as I reflected on my own family's stories, my mother's Holocaust history. I felt a connection to all the people whose voices I heard in the interviews, to the people I would never know as well as those who were part of my roots, those I loved with the very fabric of my soul. Being in Europe, I felt closer to

Poland, to my mother's roots, to her essence, a closeness I had never experienced.

A few months after listening to the French Holocaust stories, I became ill. I lost weight and became so weak I could barely walk. The out-patient doctors I visited could not find the problem. One morning, a dear friend called and told me she would pick me up and take me to the Emergency Room at the American Hospital of Paris. I weighed 86 pounds, and I was so ill that speaking was almost impossible. The on-call gastroenterologist who would be my doctor, was Jewish. I was quickly hooked up to an IV, and for the first few days, I could not eat. I slept fitfully. At night, I had dreams that I was in line to be gassed, having been labeled unfit to survive because of my fragility. Flashbacks of the Holocaust interviews entered my mind, the memories of the survivors telling their stories of their families, those lost in the camps, the sensitive souls who were the first to be killed.

I told the doctor I did not think I would make it. I really thought I would never leave that hospital alive. I was terrified.

He looked at me straight in the eyes and said *"Madame, si vous ne survivez pas, alors moi non plus."* (Roughly translated as: "Madam, if you go, I will go, too.")

Then he left the room with those words that shook me. To this day, they still shake me. Dr. Z. was convinced I would get better. He was the Jewish hero I needed at that time, the one who would reassure me that the angst and the horror in my own family's past were shared. I never told him I was Jewish, never told him of the Holocaust interviews I had listened to. I never told him of my family's past. I do not have a Jewish surname, but I do have a Jewish nose. Perhaps he sensed I was Jewish, or perhaps he never sensed it at all. Whatever his understanding was of me, as a physician, and a good one, he reminded me that we are never to forget that we are not alone in dealing with our own crises.

I thought about his words for hours, days, and then I spoke to the head nurse. I still had no appetite. She told me I was worrying too much, and instead of worrying about not eating, I should talk to my friend at dinnertime. My friend was a fellow violinist with whom I shared a stand in the orchestra. She came to visit me every day right after work and brought Ritz crackers that she munched on. Because I was not hungry, I gave her my dinner. Then, I took the head nurse's advice and talked to my friend about the orchestra we played in, her work, Paris. Gradually, I ate more of my own food and gave her less. We laughed as we both realized she was going away hungry as I was starting to gain weight.

The doctor was continually perplexed as to the cause of my illness. He had run all kinds of blood and stool tests and a colonoscopy. He tried a range of medications that did not seem to make a difference, and finally found a prescription antacid that appeared to calm things down. I started to gain weight and feel better. After ten days, I left the hospital, and because I was still quite weak, I left France and the teacher training program I was in. As soon as I landed back home in the US, I immediately got worse. I went to more doctors. Finally, a year and a half later, in 2006, I found another GI specialist, who discovered that I had a parasite growing in my intestines. He told me that the reason I most probably did not test positive for parasites before, was that in general, doctors use tests that are based on the standard size adult. Because I am a small person, my results always had come back negative, he thought. And although I will never know for sure, I believe I got this parasite from the food I was eating in my charming, yet old, apartment in Paris, that had a refrigerator that did not get very cold.

Finally, with a five-day course of antibiotics, the parasite went away, and I resumed my life, my health finally returning to me.

Once diagnosed, the parasite was simple to treat. Yet I always have viewed this parasite as a metaphor for what grows inside the psyche of the survivors and the children of survivors of severe trauma, the passing down of a legacy of a maimed world, a hole burnt in the heart of a family, a hole that continues for generation after generation.

* * *

A fragile being. That is what I have always been. So often I feel like a delicate flower, a wildflower, a wild iris, perhaps, one which needs just the right soil, just the right light, just the right temperature to bloom. If all the conditions are not met, then havoc reigns, I do not bloom, there is no flower, but only the longing to bear one. If indeed there is a flower, then it only lasts for a moment, a week perhaps, and then the petals fall, and one must wait for the following year for there to be the potential for another bloom.

My little vulnerable world cannot handle trauma, and when something disturbing affects it, I wither and need to isolate for long periods of time to recover. My body is the vessel for this vulnerability. More than five decades after I was born, I was diagnosed with fibromyalgia, a condition that results from trauma and loss, and in most cases, multiple losses, often which are quite severe in nature. I have read that it is possible for fibromyalgia to develop from intergenerational trauma, whereby a parent or a grandparent who has had a catastrophic life experience, without even knowing it, can pass the insidious effects of this trauma onto their children and their children's children. The progeny from the ensuing generations, because they have been removed from the actual trauma itself, can therefore often feel the impact of it in profound, implicit, and extremely debilitating ways.

I am not a Holocaust survivor, but I am the daughter of one, who, for her entire life, out of survival, repressed her feelings, and in doing so, unconsciously passed rage and fear and grief onto me, her most vulnerable child.

Research has shown that accumulated grief and loss can settle into a person's body over the years. That person, going about their daily life, often does not even sense that there is anything wrong, and thus has no conscious awareness of these feelings. My mother felt it was her task to survive and to create a happy life for her children. Never did she think that her past would affect her children.

Fibromyalgia is the result of a collapse at some point, from so much of this accumulated loss, the weight of it too immense for any one person to bear. The body's memory is vast and subtle, but quite vigorous. Interestingly, my mother never developed fibromyalgia, but her sister, much later in her life, did. Her sister was much younger, and therefore more impressionable when the trauma occurred.

I have learned that there is a major dysfunction in the pain-processing systems in fibromyalgia, and the nervous system becomes hyper-reactive to stimuli. As a result, pain hurts more, hot is hotter, loud is louder. People with fibromyalgia have more nerve receptors that send pain messages to the brain. This condition renders a person stuck in the sympathetic nervous system so that the hypothalamus can't stop sending danger signals to the body.

Sometimes I compare my condition to a wild horse, untamable, unruly, an out-of-control expression of this intergenerational transmission of the horrendous abuse my family faced. Fibromyalgia so often occurs when the heart is overwhelmed with painful information and sends signals to the brain that mimic and exacerbate this traumatic stress.

I didn't always have fibromyalgia, but I believe that for all the years I was growing up absorbing my mother's painful story, watching her disengage from it, I was, without knowing it, setting the stage for trauma in my own body. My inherent fragility was a breeding ground for the later onset.

This beginning occurred right after my father died, and two days later, my mother almost did too. She was with me in the kitchen, and she had a seizure. Had I not held her hand and called out her name over and over, ushering her back to the world of the living, I might have lost her, too.

There were three moments in my mother's life when I witnessed her overcome with grief and loss: the death of her father, in 1975, when I saw her cry for the first time; the death of her mother in 1991, when I witnessed in her a kind of dissolution of the psyche, a loss of sense of self; and in 2014, when her husband for sixty years passed over without her. In the latter experience, I had the feeling she was truly overwrought with a sense of abandonment. Her husband's death seemed almost too much for her to bear in her older age. She was eighty-four. After the passing of my father, she began to decline and developed dementia that got progressively worse with each year. Her health became very precarious, and she needed 24-hour care to keep her alive and at home, where she felt settled.

When her younger sister died suddenly at 86, as my mother was nearly 94 and almost completely demented, we, as a family, decided to never tell her. We knew that if we did, the floodgates would open, and she would most probably go over the edge. Her repressed feelings of so many decades would most likely finally catch up with her and kill her, likely in the form of massive heart attack, akin to the kind her father had so many years earlier.

But back to the week after my father died, that day my mother almost succumbed to the end of her existence, and I held her hand that was worn with the memory of so much loss. In that unforgettable moment, I experienced the start of my own emotional and physical crisis that my doctor would later diagnose as fibromyalgia. It was bizarre: I was carrying laundry up the stairs, as I had done dozens of times. But this time though, my body seized up and the pain was so severe I could barely move. A few weeks later, this severity did die down, but what remained was a body I no longer recognized and that I had to somehow get to know. It was now a body that would always be in pain and would need constant vigilance about everything I did, so I would not end up in the severe state I found myself in after my father passed and my mother almost vanished in front of my eyes.

The insidious thing is that no one really can heal from fibromyalgia. There is no cure that can take it away. It is a medical condition that one can monitor and understand and there are things that can help to minimize potential flare ups, but there is no way to get rid of what the body has said yes to, even if the psyche wants to will it away.

The day that my mother experienced being torn away from her home, from all that represented stability, normalcy, and congruency, into a world where survival from horrors that would become her existence, was the day the seed was planted, that would germinate years later and would end up creating a life of torment after torment for her youngest daughter.

Chapter Sixteen

More than half of the approximately 10,000 Polish civilians who found a way to leave the Russian Gulag to join the Polish army found refuge in Africa. Most landed in the former British East Africa: Uganda, Kenya, Tanganyika, (now Tanzania), North Rhodesia, (now Zambia), and South Rhodesia (now Zimbabwe), and the Cape Land in the South African Union (now the Republic of South Africa). Poles came from Tehran in British ships between May 1942 and December 1943, arriving in Mombasa, Dar Es Salaam, Tanganyika, and various ports in Mozambique and Kenya. British commanders decided where to house the Polish refugees, and often would transport them far from the port cities where they landed. Overall, there were nineteen Polish settlements scattered around Africa. All of those were developed, managed, and maintained by the British. Hospitals and schools were created for the refugees. Demographically, in the camps, 47% were women, 11.5% men, and 41.5 % children and teenagers. Most of the latter was female as adolescent boys were generally in military schools in Palestine or Egypt. Included in the 11.5% men, were adults who were too old or ill to serve in the military. Most of the camps were made up of single women and their children, as the men were off in Europe or North Africa fighting in the war. The greater part of the refugees was Catholic (approximately 90%) and only a handful were Jewish (approximately 5%). The remaining were Greek Orthodox.

In December 1942, after a four-week ship voyage, Andrzej and his family arrived in Mombasa, the main port in Kenya. Polish officials directed the refugees to camps in East Africa, giving each family a choice of camps. Andrzej and Gosia chose Tanganyika because they were told it had the best climate. The families boarded trains to their new settlement. They arrived a week later in Tengeru, in the middle of the jungle, in the shadow of Mount Meru. In the distance they could see Mount Kilimanjaro, the highest peak in Africa, at 19,341 feet.

They were shown their homes, round huts made of mud with conical banana-leaf roofs and dirt floors. There were a few buildings made of stone that were assigned to the camp hospital, the quarters for the British camp commandant and the British administration facilities.

In her flight from Poland, Gosia did not take any of her teaching documents. Coincidentally, on the ship to Africa, she had met a colleague from Cracow who had been a teacher in the same high school where she had taught. At that time, in 1942, he was a member of the Polish Administration in Nairobi, and he was visiting the Polish refugee camps. Gosia asked him for a statement indicating that he had known her as teacher. Because of his prestigious position, he was able to produce a certificate with an official stamp that would allow her to teach in Tengeru.

An education advisor, Mr. Szczepanski, who had been chairman of the Board of Education in Cracow, offered Gosia the position of principal of the newly formed high school. Gosia did not accept the position. She was the only Jewish teacher, and her daughter Ewa was the only Jewish student, and she did not want to assume the responsibility of one thousand Catholic students. All her colleagues tried to persuade her to take the position, but she did not back down from her decision. All she wanted to do was be a conscientious teacher. She was hired to teach English and Latin. She became, very quickly, the most valued and appreciated teacher in the high school and she had an excellent rapport with all her students.

Andrzej drove around the camp in a car that was given to him by the camp commandant. He regularly inspected the conditions of the huts and other structures for damage. Everything made from wood had to be checked for termites, who could easily destroy a building in minutes. He learned Swahili and worked with the native population and gave them jobs as they maintained the camp and constructed new buildings. They built a Catholic church, a Greek Orthodox church, and a Jewish synagogue.

There were about twenty Jews who went to the synagogue each week for prayers on Fridays. Not being very pious, still, Gosia and Andrzej clung to their Jewish identity and hoped their children would as well. Agnieszka was proud of the synagogue her father had built and told her Catholic friends that she too had a little "church." Ewa, on the other hand, had little interest in it.

* * *

Ewa was twelve years old when she arrived in Tengeru. She had been a war refugee for three years, a quarter of her life. Her head bore very short hair, that was beginning to grow back after being shaved off due to lice. She had no idea what was in store for her. During those three years, she had numbed herself from the tragedies that had befallen her and her family, from the day the bombs fell to the present. She looked around at the new and unknown territory that would be their home, in the middle of the jungle. She saw only mattresses on the dirt floor to sleep on, with mosquito netting to prevent malaria. She watched her bewildered mother almost cry. She knew they were free, but so far away from anything that resembled what they knew. In her young life, she was made aware that they did not have any control over their destiny.

Within a few days after their arrival, she and her family started to get infections in the toenails, due to a soil-dwelling parasite that buried itself under the nails. They then laid eggs and caused painful infections to the host. They had to learn how to remove the egg sacs without puncturing them.

They were told not to go out in the sun without lined hats, to be wary of pythons and other deadly snakes and to not drink the water without boiling it first. Everything was different from anything they had ever known. Animals, plants, food, and climate were all foreign. Ewa did what she had done best for three years: keep her feelings inside and adapt.

A school was formed by the British and she entered the sixth grade. Polish textbooks were sent overseas by the British and every day she went to a barrack-like building to immerse herself in the first school she had been to in three years. She made friends, became fearless of snakes, drank the water in the springs without boiling it first and without getting sick or dying.

One of the friends she made was named Marysia who was in Tengeru without her family. When the Russians came to deport families from Poland, they took everyone in the house. Marysia was visiting a friend at the time. That family was deported to Siberia and the Russian guards took her with them. She never saw her family again. Later, she would learn that her entire family had been killed.

Another girl, Jadwiga, thought the world of Ewa, because she was so good, so sweet, and seemingly so unfettered by the ills of the world. They became instant friends, did many things together, and they could talk for hours with each other. It was a friendship that would last their entire lives, even after Jadwiga eventually migrated to London after the war. With Jadwiga, Ewa felt special, unjudged, and she used to tell her that she wished all friends could be like her.

All of Ewa's friends were Catholics. She and her sister were the only Jewish children in the camp. There were only a handful of Jewish adults who were elderly men. She desperately wanted to fit in, but this could never happen, due to the antisemitism that existed in the camp of 4000 people. She tried to convince herself that she did not want to be a part of the Girl Scouts, but secretly longed to be allowed to join this group to which all her friends belonged, and to which her application was denied. She asked Marysia if she learned to cross herself, would she be accepted. She did not want to be different than the norm. All her friends did their chores on Saturdays and then got dressed up on Sundays to go to church. Ewa tried to do this, except she had nowhere to go on Sundays. When her mother found out that she was doing this, she made her do her chores on Sundays and resented the fact that her daughter wanted to defy her Jewishness.

One day, she allowed her feelings to surface, the rage she felt for not just being different, but for all the moments in her preadolescent life where she was thrown into situations that were subhuman, being made to feel like a criminal when she had done nothing wrong.

She tried to run away from home.

But she had nowhere to go. The camp was dark at night and the noises from the neighboring jungle terrified her.

She came home and resumed her life of repressed emotions that would be the theme she would hold inside for decades and decades.

Agnieszka was just five years old when the family arrived in Tanganyika. Her most formative preschool years had been spent as a prisoner, as a refugee, as a victim of something her young brain could never have understood. However, deeply lasting impressions were made during those preverbal and early verbal years, when survival was the only theme. Her world was flooded with anxiety, chaos, and loss. Had it not been for Agata, she would probably later have developed a severe emotional disability. Agata was the most important person in her life and was more of a mother to her during those precarious early years than her own mother ever could be.

Many experiences the family had Agnieszka would not remember, yet her young brain would store everything in the unconscious. One of her first vague memories was when she was in the back of the truck during the escape from Radom and Agata was singing to her. Then, we fast forward a few years and her first clear memory was on the ship to Karachi from Iran. Agnieszka was snuggled up against Agata on the ship in the cargo hold. It was packed with people and belongings, and filth and noise were prevalent. She remembered being cozy and comfortable in her nanny's arms, seemingly far away from the cacophony of the world around her.

When the family first arrived in Tengeru, Tanganyika, everyone lived in one single hut. But after a few months, they moved to a pair of new huts. Then Agata got her own hut. Agnieszka missed her terribly and visited her often, spending more time with Agata than with her own family nearby. She remembered the freshly baked bread that she always seemed to have. Agata would often make her fresh bread with butter and onion sandwiches, so Agnieszka would come home stinking of onions, which her father detested.

Agata met a man, a widower with two teenage children, got married and had a baby girl. After that, things were no longer the same, as she had her own child to care for. Agnieszka did not see her as much, as she did not care for this man she married and felt that Agata's energies now were focused on the man's children as well as her own little baby.

Feeling abandoned, she instead immersed herself in trying to grow up in a refugee camp. Five years later, in September 1947, when she was ten years old, she and her father left Tengeru for Dar es Salaam, where her father had found a new job as a paid engineer. Her sister had stayed in Tengeru to finish high school, with their mother who also needed to finish her teaching assignment. Living in a Polish refugee camp in a single room barrack with a corrugated metal roof with no screen door, she was invaded by heat, insects, and loneliness. She had no friends, her father was away working much of the time and, because she did not speak English, she was put back in first grade classes. She would never return to Tengeru and would never see Agata again. For many years, she would cry when she remembered her, knowing she had lost her.

* * *

While Ewa mostly had nothing to do with her Jewish identity, Agnieszka, in her young middle childhood mind, got glimpses of aspects she hated, and aspects she pondered scrupulously.

When she was still in Tengeru, Agnieszka went with her parents (without Ewa, who refused to go) to the synagogue for Passover. The few Jewish men in the camp intoned in Hebrew, which Agnieszka did not understand. She became thoroughly bored and restless with the hours and hours of Hebrew prayers before the meal. But the matzos and the sweet wine appealed to her before she was allowed to be excused from the table. At Yom Kippur, she felt ensconced by the eerie glow of the single large yahrzeit candle. It was the one day of the year where her mother allowed herself to cry at the memory of those who had died, most specifically her own mother's death when she was so young. Agnieszka stared at the candle and imagined the spirits of the dead being drawn to it like moths. The candle and all that it represented terrified her.

For her, the worst part of being Jewish was walking to and from school. As she made this trek every day, boys in the camp who came from the orphanage would constantly call her names, laugh at her and spit and urinate in her direction. She became terrified of walking to school. Those names and the mean gestures would wear onto her like a filthy rag that had been shoved inside her heart. Terrified as she was, she never told her parents about this until much later, when she was an adult.

Fear permeated Agnieszka in those impressionable childhood years. Within each block of huts there was a communal outhouse, a dark, smelly, fly-infested building with several open stalls. There was an opening in the cement floor where one had to squat. The smell was nauseating, and she was afraid she would fall in. There was no toilet paper. Some lucky people had old newspapers. After dark, she was terrified of going to the outhouse, so she didn't. She was allowed to pee in the dirt by their huts, but when she had to have a bowel movement, she held it in, which caused her great abdominal distress.

One day, Agnieszka woke up to a clear sky. It was sunny and beautiful. But the unpredictability of the jungle, a metaphor for her early years, crept up and invaded the landscape of her home, her brain, her life. Suddenly, the sky turned extremely dark with what seemed like clouds, but there were swarms of locusts that blocked out the sun.

Locusts invaded the camps, decimating every plant in sight and miles of cornfields.

Her father, her heroic father, saved the family many times over. He was a risk taker, sometimes endangering the very lives he saved. When he was not immersed in his work, he ruled the family with a few polarized beliefs, where things were either right or wrong. It was wrong to lie, right to give money to a relative, wrong to spend money on ice cream, or meals in a restaurant. He had no patience for weakness or fear. Tears made him angry. There was no such thing as emotional or psychological distress. When one had physical pain, there were two remedies: aspirin or castor oil. When Agnieszka was still rather young, she had shooting pains in her abdomen. Andrzej, according to his two-dimensional theory, gave her a spoonful of castor oil. She immediately vomited it all up. Less than an hour later, she was rushed to the hospital in Dar es Salaam, where she was living with her father at the time and had an emergency appendectomy. The doctors later told her that had she not vomited, the castor oil treatment could have killed her.

When she finally left Africa to come to America, Agnieszka never felt any excitement, joy, or dismay. It was just the next journey for her in this life where things happened beyond her control, and she was only like a leaf in the wind. And mostly, the wind was stronger than the leaf.

* * *

Gosia never knew that a loaf of bread would save her life. But then again, she never knew that she would be in a jungle in Tanganyika. She looked down at the ground, the dry, dusty earth. The ants had invaded it again. They came in hordes, unannounced, hundreds of thousands of them, half the size of her thumb, each one following the next. She watched their crawling bodies, heading away from her. They were hungry and they seemed to be marching towards a neighbor's hut. When their bellies were empty, as was so often the case, they could consume someone's entire home in a mere two hours, their crunching sounds audible from a sizable distance. She wanted to run, to forewarn her neighbor and her family to come quickly, but when she tried to get up, she was so weak, and her body could not move. Her head spun, and she slowly fell into a dizzying dreamless sleep.

A week before, alone in the teachers' lunchroom, she had heard the news. Every day normally, she and all the other faculty members listened to the BBC, reporting from London. That day though, the radio, their one link to the world, had stopped working and the frustrated teachers had left the room. Gosia had stayed, hoping that the radio would miraculously somehow find its voice. It did, minutes after her colleagues had vanished. In one singular statement, the Cambridge accent unveiled the news. As Gosia sat on the hard- back chair, listening, alone, Hitler's mania loomed ominously in front of her; the reality of Auschwitz was revealed. The reporter continued in a somber tone as he read the bulletin: millions so far had perished in the gas chambers...

Gosia had put her head in her hands and wailed as she thought of all the Jews stolen, gassed and obliterated.

* * *

No one was there to comfort her, but had the others been there, callousness would have reigned. To the other teachers, it would have been a shocking story, but it would not have affected them personally, and most likely would have funneled even more wariness toward Jews. They tolerated Gosia, and even made friends with her, because of her brilliance and the fact that her students loved her, but mostly they were on her side because her husband, one of the few men in the camp, fixed everything, and the women all needed him at some time. He was handsome, intelligent and kind, and the women all missed their own husbands, fighting on the front lines, oceans away. They flirted with him and ignored that he was happily married with two children and that he was, indeed, Jewish.

* * *

Before the BBC came on, while she was sitting on her hard chair in the empty room, Gosia had pondered her lecture that day, on Samuel Beckett's *Waiting for Godot.* She had always loved that play. Its simplicity foreshadowed all, she felt.

"The tears of the world are a constant quantity. For each one who begins to weep somewhere else another stops... There is man in his entirety, blaming his shoe when his foot is guilty... I'm like that. Either I forget right away, or I never forget."

She had talked about these three lines for most of the class. She wanted her students to think about the war, to consider what war was; she wanted them to explore the act of blame, she wanted them to feel united in this world, and in doing so, to cry collectively. She wanted them to move past labels of Jewish and not Jewish, to put hatred forever aside, and she wanted them to never forget atrocities that humans' assault on each other. Before listening to the radio later that morning, she had wanted her students to know the truth in all its haunting shades. Her students at first had been quiet, reserved. They had been waiting for Godot, she thought out loud, for a person who would never come, for someone who would take care of them, a God, perhaps. She had wanted them to be that Godot, to speak up and to speak eloquently, with as much intelligence in their brains as compassion in their hearts.

They hadn't been able to do so. Their silence had been deafening.

Then, the one in the back, the little blond girl, Marysia, spoke up. She had never said a word all year. It was rumored that her mother had been having relations with an African man from across the river. Marysia had been shunned by her peers because of this possibility, not even knowing if it was true. Her voice had wavered.

"Professor Majewski, I believe you are talking about the silent Godot." She stopped; her quiet voice became silent. Gosia nodded for her to continue.

"Every time there is a pause in society, a silence in what needs to be said, we are all silencing Godot, the figure that never comes. We are like sheep, afraid to bleat, afraid to stand up for what is not right, for injustice. We forget right away, our minds become distracted. We blame so easily, before we even look at ourselves and our silence which is made up of our hostile game. I feel the tears around the world. Look at what is happening that we, in our little jungle, are afraid to look at. Will we walk away from it, scoffing its credulity, or will we look at our own Godots and cry with all the rest?"

Marysia sat down, shaking from her words. The class was silent and stared down at their feet. Gosia stood, her hands on her hips and shook her head. She smiled and shook her head again, amazed at her student's brilliance, the insights that poured out of that small being, the fire in her belly that inspired life.

She loved teaching, those moments when it is not about the teacher, but when the students, their minds, their hearts, splay open; when they get it, and they leap. They dive into a lake. They are tentative at first, their arms outstretched, their steps bouncing, and then they do it, following the curve of the body, the line of a perfect arc into the water.

Teaching had taken her away from the world, even if she had been instructing her students to be a part of it.

After Marysia spoke there was a rumble in the classroom. Silence had prevailed for a few moments until Irinia, a robust teenager, muscle emanating from her thighs, had stood.

"We were not raised to think this way, Professor. We were told to be complacent. Look at us, we are displaced from our country and our homes were stolen from us. Our fathers are dying on the front lines, there is *no* Godot. We are not waiting for a ghost that will never arrive. We were taught to hate, to judge, to take for ourselves. When our fathers are gone, and we are stuck with our mothers to raise us, what will we know then? Where will we go after this? My little sister barely remembers Poland. All she knows is our grass huts and the banana trees. I see a better world, one where we have the power to not wait for what does not make sense."

Gosia, her small frame illuminated by the sun that poured through the window, again nodded her head, wanting more.

Bronek, in the back, begged for his entrance.

"We were taught to hate Jews, "he began, stirring up the class, their heads fixed on him. "I know what is happening over there in Europe. They think we're dummies, like we are not supposed to know the truth. They are killing them, hundreds of thousands, maybe even millions of Jews, slaughtering them, rounding them up and thinking this is the final solution to making a better world. They think we are supposed to believe this. Then they, like you read to us, tell us to blame our shoes when our feet are guilty. Then they run away, with smiles on their faces. It is disgusting, this world is disgusting, the lies are disgusting. Why do we have to hate, except for those who hate? If I were German, I would be killing people right now. I would be part of the Hitler Juden, the young who are forced into a world of propagating hatred and I wouldn't have a choice. Thank God, I am Polish, and I am here, but what good is it to be safe, to be a refugee, when the world around me is threatened, is perishing, at the mercy of one despicable man. We came here, all of us, quiet and meek, scared and squirming. Now, we are different. We have all changed, we have come of age in Tanganyika, and we have you as the most influential teacher we have ever had and most probably ever will have."

He sat down and folded his hands. The bell rang, and class was over. One by one the students filed out. They were looking down, their faces afraid to show what had just happened in class that day. When the room was silent, and Gosia was alone with the echo of the words that had just been spoken, she began to shake, her heart raw with emotions. She looked at the now empty desks lined up across from her, the energy still in the wood reflecting the minds that housed compassion, that screamed out for change in their blighted world.

* * *

Gosia put her head in her hands and wailed. She was alone, in the teacher's lunchroom. Her class, the discussion, the philosophy of mankind were the last things on her mind now. *Millions of Jews gassed, they reported. Philosophy will never explain this. My father, my brother, my grandparents, my in-laws, my cousins, my aunts, and uncles. Gone. Why me?*

Her mind raced, the guilt of survival overcame all the facts and figures that had been reported. As the midday heat smothered life around her, she shuddered in her hands, feeling her breath, her vile breath against her skin.

I should be there with them, perishing together, why did I escape?

She forgot then about her husband, her two children. Nothing mattered anymore as she trudged back home to her empty hut. With no more classes to teach that day, she went to her mattress on the packed earthen floor and cried. She never cried. Her tears felt foreign, and her head spun in a myriad of directions.

She could not imagine living anymore. Hearing the truth, knowing it now, made her sick. Life was nothing. Her family, and millions of others were gone in the flames of one person's madness. She fell asleep, a restless sleep until her husband and children came home. Then, she slept harder, and they could not wake her. In the morning, when she still had not woken up, Andrzej called the doctor. He diagnosed her with the flu and prescribed sleep. When the family had left for work and school, she opened her eyes and lay motionless in her bed. She rolled over, feeling hunger pains.

Now, all is different. I no longer wish to call myself a survivor.

She felt her throat close as she envisioned her brother, her beloved brother, gassed, his own breath suffocated, his sweet laughter stolen forever. She had a vision of him, the last time she saw him, when her youngest was just born. He was so happy holding his tiny niece in his strong arms, as if she were a leaf and he was the tree. He whispered something in her ear. She always wondered what he had said.

She began to moan, hunger mixed in with a haunting mournful wail for all the dead, for all the corpses laid out in her mind's eye. She stared out the window of the hut and her distorted vision saw millions of ants on the ground, troops on the front lines heading towards her, approaching fast and faster. Her breathing became rapid, and then her brother appeared in a vision. He stomped them out with his big, thick boots. He wore a Star of David around his neck, and he laughed; the sounds lingered and echoed throughout the camp. He lifted his sister in his arms, as they fled the camp and ran through the savannah and away.

I must be dying. It is time.

She felt her skin, how it had lost its softness, dry and brittle now, parched and without fluid. She could barely open her mouth; her lips were cracked and starved. She closed her eyes, waited and groaned.

Hitler brought me to this place.

Her thoughts turned to that man, and she convulsed, her body wracked with the poison of his being. She could not push him away. She tried to get him out of her thoughts, but still he prevailed, his insidious smile curved at the corners, spewing fire out of his eyes.

Gosia tried to turn over in her bed. She tried to rid his image away from torturing her, but she could not move. Weakness had taken over her body and she had no choice but to succumb to it. She closed her eyes and let sleep fill her beleaguered brain, a restless, starved sleep full of demons and monsters, who crept in and tried to devour every one of her muscles and bones. She tried to scream, but nothing came out but her own gagged silence.

* * *

Later that afternoon, as the sun waned and the trees swayed gently with the first of the evening breezes, she heard a sound.

There were incessant knocks on the door.

She tried to ignore them.

They became louder and sounded like bullets to her head. She groaned. Her hunger had turned her into something primitive.

Footsteps approached her. Her cloudy vision could see only vague forms. She could not speak.

Their faces drawn and worried, her students held it to her nose. A fresh loaf of bread they had just made. They had spent all day at it, missed their classes, fumbled with the recipe and had stolen ingredients from the camp kitchen. They had watched their mothers make bread in Poland, and they tried to make a loaf from the old ways, using their elbows to check for the correct oven temperature.

Gosia thought they were apparitions and continued her moaning. The students didn't leave, they waved the freshly baked bread under her nose and watched the steam rise, the flavors of the rye and the wheat mixing with the yeast, wafting through the air.

Gosia ceased her guttural sounds and became silent. Her nose twitched. The scent of the bread filled it.

Her mouth instinctively opened.

Her students excitedly tore off a piece, a tiny crumb, and gently placed it on their teacher's tongue.

Her mouth closed. The crumb dissolved. Again, she opened her mouth, and the students broke off a slightly larger piece of bread and placed it into the awaiting vessel of life.

As the sun drifted behind the trees, creating shadows and a darkened room, the students continued. Her mouth opened, their beloved professor's mouth, and they, the adoring students, fed her, bite by bite.

They watched her, moment by moment, return to life.

She first regained vision. From the smells to the tastes, now she could see what it was she was eating. Bread, the staff of life, moved its way, like a snake, into the underbelly of her conscious self, to the vast array of transcendent waves and connected her to a force that went beyond guilt, grief and beyond the agony of what humans do to each other, to a place that chooses survival once again.

She opened her eyes and managed to put on a small smile.

"We almost lost you, dear Professor," Marysia said. Her dark eyes pierced the small space.

"Why did you want to leave us?" Bronek asked.

"I didn't want to leave you. I didn't want to leave anyone. It's just sometimes the world is so ugly." She looked into their hopeful eyes. She often wondered who needed whom more.

Maybe at the end of the day, teaching is all about feeding hungry mouths and being fed back.

She took one last big bite of bread and savored each morsel. The doughy piece slid down into her almost satiated belly.

She rose and her students took her by the hand and watched her feet touch the earth.

"Please, don't tell my family."

Her students nodded. It would be their secret that they saved the life of their beloved teacher. They led her outside. It was early evening. Her husband and her two daughters were just coming home. In the distance, frogs and crickets sang in a chorus. The blooming datura flowers around them spread their intoxicating evening scents.

Survival was everywhere, the pulsing and constantly changing actions of living beings.

Chapter Seventeen

My grandparents arrived in the United States in 1950. They ended up in Berkeley, California where a cousin of my grandfather's had sponsored them. A few years later, they decided to buy a house.

My grandfather had been offered a good job as a structural engineer at Bechtel Engineering and in their house hunt, they approached a part of the Bay Area that would embody their dreams: a place in the San Francisco East Bay hills that would be resplendent with diamonds… the lights of the city … and hope for a good life immune from strife. In 1957 they found a magnificent home, built only a few decades earlier that had a panoramic view of the Bay and San Francisco. My grandparents fell instantly in love with this house where the night lights did shine like diamonds and where they felt transported to an existence where their blighted past felt far away. They first saw the house at sunset, and they fell under its spell: the infinite beauty when the colors of the sky reflect on the bay and everything looks like it is burning, then the lights emerge to form a magical landscape.

I spent many days and overnights at this house with my grandparents, and, after my grandfather passed, with my grandmother. I loved being there.

Every year, at Passover, we sat at the oval teak table in the grand dining room that overlooked the bay. We were always dressed up for the occasion. We went around the table and each of us would read a section of the Haggadah. When we came to the Dayenu's, my grandmother would put down the Haggadah, take off her glasses and speak to us with a serious tone. Every year she would say the same thing:

"Isn't it enough that we survived Hitler? Isn't it enough that we survived Siberia and the African jungle? Isn't it enough that we survived every single hardship that was handed to us? Isn't it enough that our children came out of all the hardships healthy in body and spirit? Isn't it enough that Andrzej has a good job, and we have a beautiful home?"

We would all say after that: *"Dayenu."*

And then in a quiet voice she would add: *"Were we better human beings than our brothers and sisters who perished in the gas chambers?"*

Once a year I would remember what happened in my family's history and the severity of my grandmother's tone reminded us of something awful. But in that once-a-year moment, I would look at my mother and see an expressionless face, one which seemed to imply that nothing bad happened to our family and the dead ones were gone, so don't spend too much energy thinking about them. I veered towards this attitude, as it was simpler. As I said the obligatory *Dayenu*, it was, like my mother, without emotion.

I remember a very small part of me, however, would always gulp a tiny bit when my grandmother, my Baba as we called her, reminded us of this juxtaposition of gratefulness and guilt, that survivor guilt I was brought up with, perhaps the one feeling I was allowed to feel. I know many Jewish survivors experience this. The "why me?" perspective. We, as descendants of the survivors, had not ever heard a bomb, had not ever had to have our heads shaved for lice, had not ever had to live behind barbed wires, had not ever had to be starving, had not ever had to be crammed into inhuman, barbaric conditions that supported a psychology of survival of trauma…all because of our religion, our ethnicity and our geography. Bereft of the emotional impact of their situations, still, we, as descendants of the survivors, had been fed, since early childhood, stories of escape, stories of heroism, stories of luck and stories of amazing endurance. These stories made up dinner conversations night after night in our family. On Passover, whether we took it in or not, we were given the opportunity every year to reflect on the *Dayenu* of survival, and we were reminded of the horrors that were just on the other side of the fence in our family, in millions of other families, the horrors of so many people who perished. Upon reflection, decades later, of this knowledge, I saw that my grandmother was sharing with us her grief, a not-be-named eternal sadness, a constant reminder of loss, of just how close we, in our family, are to loss, something intangible that we feel in the throbbing of our veins, a life-impeding loss that just never goes away. This loss is connected to guilt, the guilt of surviving, of being alive. In this way, joy and sadness are intrinsically woven together.

What we, as descendants of survivors, also learned was that our parents and grandparents adjusted to the dailiness, to the status quo of life, rather than to the hardships. To be a survivor, we learned, was to not talk about the pain, to not express it, and to not let it overcome our lives. What the survivors never told us was that this pain never disappears and instead gets transmitted to the next generation, the one that never heard a bomb in the middle of the night.

As a child and adolescent, I never spoke of these issues, these feelings, I never wrote about them, I never pondered them. I didn't even know they were there. I just lived, holding onto, and turning inward, my family's grief and trauma. It became my depression, and, eventually, my fibromyalgia. For so many years, all this energy was bursting inside me, like a sun that never sets, but boils up with energy that has nowhere to go.

* * *

Another salient part of the Passover Seder was that my mother truly hated it. She went through the motions of sitting at the table every year, reading from the Haggadah when it was her turn to read and nodding her head when it was her turn to nod. She did it for her parents, and later her mother, when her father was no longer alive. She did it because not to do it would be an act of rebellion, and she had never rebelled in her life.

She hated Passover, but really, she hated being Jewish. For her, being Jewish meant that her whole life was destroyed. From those first instances as a child in the woods with her friend, cutting down the tree and bringing it inside for Christmas, her father raging, to all the Holocaust experiences she had to endure as a child and adolescent, she created in her mind a reality that connected being Jewish with hatred of oneself. Freedom, for her, meant to not be Jewish. Going further with this notion, she felt that if you are not Jewish, then your life could be happy. She thought if she married a non-Jew, raised her children to not be of any religion, if she never mentioned the word Jewish to her children, then she could start over and have a good life, the one she perhaps envisioned for herself there in the woods that day, when she was so young and impressionable, when already there was tension in the air in Eastern Europe.

Unfortunately, there were several layers of problems with my mother's theory. The first one was her mother and father, who were very Jewish, wanted so badly for my mother to be so as well. Of course, there were never any words addressing this matter. Just sighs. My grandmother was the queen of sighs of distaste, the quiet mechanism by which she did not approve of something. These sighs of disapproval continued at Christmas, when my mother invited her over for dinner and presents, the latter of which were put under the freshly cut decorated Christmas tree which my mother treasured year after year. My grandmother would always sit next to the tree because that was where the heater vent was, as she was always cold in her daughter's house. She never once looked at the tree, but instead, sighed heavily sitting next to it. As a child, I never quite understood this disapproval. I was confused as to why my mother and grandmother hated something that was so meaningful to the other. I was confused about a lot of things in my family. I was so fuzzy about these vital aspects of being human. Sometimes I felt like I wanted someone to give me a script, a synopsis, a narrative that made sense of it all.

The next layer of my mother's problematic theory concerned identity. Being Jewish was not, in my family, about being religious. On the contrary, while my grandparents went to Temple for the High Holidays, for the most part being Jewish was about identity, about who you are on this planet, about your belief system, your heritage, who you are connected to. (Incidentally, my grandfather was an atheist, and both my grandparents chose cremation after their deaths.)

When my mother decided to throw her Jewishness away, she was, I believe, throwing herself away, saying to the world that identity is not important. She told us once that she never felt she belonged. She wasn't American, she wasn't Jewish, she wasn't Polish. But then she confused me because she always said Poles were not Jewish and that her mother refused to visit Poland later in life because of their antisemitism. So, in this way, she must have identified with some aspect of being Jewish but could not admit it. I believe she raised us Jewish despite her intentions.

The more I think about it, the more I see that truly it is impossible to deny one's identity. You can make it invisible, but there is a price in trying to obliterate who you are. When I see how my mother pushed away this part of herself, she not only damaged her grasp in the world, her rootedness, but she also maimed her children's sense of self, our sense of belonging, our sense of being on the inside of the knowledge of humanness, rather than on the outside, looking in and feeling confused and overwhelmed by it all.

Then there is one final layer of my mother's ill-adapted theory, which is perhaps the most insidious. Being Jewish meant trauma. It meant displacement. It meant being thrown into the category of the worst of the worst of humanity, being tortured and given a life that wasn't a life but was mostly surviving not life, i.e., death. How can anyone have explained that to my mother when she was a young child/ adolescent, a girl who just wanted to grow up from pig tails swinging in the breeze to having friends over, to finding love, adventure, a home, a profession, and in the midst, cultivating joy in just being alive?

Two of my mother's daughters, my sister and I, had Jewish weddings. Her two grandchildren, my nieces, had bat mitzvahs. My mother was quite happy to celebrate these family events, but she experienced no joy about the Jewish aspect of them, and in fact, she openly expressed a deep-down sense of dread before and during those four occasions. *How could Jewishness be celebrated?* she seemed to ask herself. She wondered aloud where she went wrong, why her children and grandchildren would *choose* to be Jewish?

Hatred of self because of Hitler and everyone else who hated Jews. That's what I think it was. This hatred instilled a poison in the essential fabric of each person who had to endure this tortured time. Those who survived had to conjure up all kinds of methods to keep going, to not succumb to the fragmentation and disintegration of a people because one man deemed it so.

Hitler and everyone else who hated Jews not only maimed, ruined and slaughtered those they touched, but generations and generations and generations of individuals after him.

My mother's theories seemed right for her, but as I tried to look at them from the inside, they seemed horribly distorted and conjured up a sense of inner shame, a disgust of self, a longing to be someone who she was not. Her silence of her real feelings only added to this distortion, for in the absence of words, there is only a transmission of this silent disgust. All her adult life she stifled her rage towards the outside, towards the demons who maimed and shattered her blooming identity.

It is the survivor's job to survive, however. My mother did her job well. How could she have known; how can any survivor know how to move beyond trauma? How can the survivors know the impact of what they are transmitting to their children when they are only focused on staying alive and trying to find a place in this world?

Chapter Eighteen

I n 1947, almost all the camps were liquidated, and by 1949, the camps were officially closed. While a few of the emigrants decided to remain in Africa, many of the residents of the camps migrated to Canada, Britain, the US, and New Zealand if they had family members or an employer who would sponsor them. Some went to Palestine. The families who were not accepted anywhere, did not want, or were unable to return to Poland, were sent by British authorities to Western Australia.

* * *

In September 1945, Gosia held in her hand a letter with an affidavit from her husband's cousin in Berkeley, California, with an official seal: her family was given permission to come to the United States of America. This cousin had found out where she was through the Red Cross. With haste, she and Andrzej went to the American Consulate in Nairobi. They told them they could get their quota number in two weeks.

Two weeks passed, then three, then a month and still no letter arrived. Andrzej went back to Nairobi. The Consulate told them a new law had just been passed, which stated that survivors of concentration camps would get priority in obtaining immigration visas. For all other applicants, there was a mandatory five-year waiting period to enter the United States.

Little by little, their camp in Tengeru was being liquidated. Military families were going back to England. Andrzej's family was given four choices: return to Poland, obtain entry permits to Australia, stay in East Africa, or immigrate to South Africa. They knew they could never return to Poland; their homeland would never accept them again. Australia was unknown and too far away. There were no jobs in East Africa. After some waiting, Andrzej obtained, through assistance from a Zionist organization, an offer to work in Johannesburg.

Meanwhile, a commission arrived at the camp to recruit young men and women for employment in Canada. Andrzej was too old. Agata, however, grabbed at the chance, and she and her new family left immediately. Gosia gave her the address of her cousin in Berkeley and asked her to let her know when she safely landed in Canada. No word from her ever came. Gosia never heard from her again.

* * *

In June 1948, after the end of the school year, Gosia and Ewa left Tengeru, and joined Agnieszka and Andrzej in Dar-es-Salaam. They stayed in a Polish temporary camp that was miserably hot. In August 1948, three years after Gosia received the affidavit from her husband's cousin, she received entry visas for her and her family to immigrate to South Africa.

One month later, they arrived in Johannesburg.

Apartheid was everywhere, juxtaposed with lush green grass, exotic flowers and wide avenues with expensive shops. In the beautiful parks, there were benches for whites, Asians, and Blacks. When they took buses, they were only allowed on the newer, fancier ones reserved for whites. When they were to take a train, there were three entrances that corresponded with one's race.

Everyone in the family was horrified about this obsession for stratification based on race. They had been forced to survive Hitler's hatred, Stalin's hatred and the world's obsession with hatred. Johannesburg's oppressive mentality suffocated them, but still they had to live and eat and sleep. Officials gave them for a short time a make-shift place to live in a run-down boarding house. Then they moved to another boarding house where they lived in one room and a large closet. Ewa and Agnieszka were ordered to learn Afrikaans in school, an ungainly language that they quickly learned, but detested.

One day Gosia went to the doctor for some numbness in her thumb.

"Are you Jewish?" he asked.

Gosia wondered why he was asking this but replied: "Yes."

The doctor then stated that the problem was not in her thumb, but in her neck where the nerve ending was. The treatment was to hang her by the neck. He put a rope around her neck. She held onto a bar. He then removed the stool she was standing on for a few seconds and told her to return to the clinic for nine additional hanging treatments.

The doctor smirked as he walked out.

* * *

In December 1949, Andrzej was summoned to the American consulate, where he was told that their quota number from Washington had arrived, and they had 48 hours to accept or reject the visa. The family had a meeting to decide what to do. Andrzej insisted that they needed to leave South Africa at once, that they were living on a powder keg, and that soon a racial war would invade all South Africa. Race riots were a daily occurrence in Sofiatown, a suburb of Johannesburg. While the family all agreed and wanted to run away as fast as they could from

South Africa, Gosia was frightened about emigrating to the United States. It was never where she wanted to end up; it was not a country that had ever appealed to her with its contradictory democracy. But her family did not agree with her, and she let her visions and dreams of moving to Israel... or anywhere else... wither away, as she went home with her family and prepared yet again to journey towards a destination that was at least, away from her experiences of the war.

* * *

On the 8th of January 1950, they left Johannesburg. They boarded the train to Cape Town where they got on a huge British ocean liner that took them across the Indian and the Atlantic Oceans. Two weeks later, they arrived in Southampton, England and were met with a different hemisphere, freezing rain and fog. The vestiges of war had not yet vanished from England, and one could only buy meagre things at shops, only with rationed coupons. They were cold, lost, and miserable, but mostly uncertain about this next stage of their lives.

One week later, they boarded the S.S. America and were on their way to New York. The Atlantic Ocean was rough and stormy, so all four of them were seasick the entire time and could not even stand up or eat. They felt wretched and longed for dry land.

Five days later, the Statue of Liberty greeted them. Gosia was not thrilled, not in the least excited or moved as her thoughts turned to her apprehension of arriving in what she perceived as a dreaded future in this strange land, this new continent. She longed to go back to Poland, to her home country that no longer existed in the way she had left it. Andrzej's cousin waited for them at the harbor, as she glanced at the suitcase and the few bundles that were all they had. They spent three days in New York in a dilapidated hotel. Gosia was overwhelmed by the traffic and the crowds in the streets.

Ewa was put on a train for Houston, Texas. She would be living with her father's recently widowed aunt and going to the University there, and she convinced her parents that it would be best to have fewer responsibilities and one less child as they tried to settle into the San Francisco Bay Area. This decision ended up being yet one more displacement for Ewa and, as it turned out, her aunt never wanted her to live with her. After four months, without any explanation, Aunt Sally put Ewa on a plane to San Francisco. Ewa was wearing a new dress that her aunt had made for her. In the distress of her life, she vomited all over this dress just as the plane was taking off. She would remember this vomit decades later.

* * *

On the 5th of February, the same day that Ewa left for Houston, Gosia, Andrzej and Agnieszka boarded the train across the country to Berkeley, California. When they arrived, cherry blossoms were beginning to show and spring was beckoning, but they did not notice.

What they did recognize was that they were at the end of a dramatically harrowing and uncertain journey that they would never forget.

The first few weeks in the Bay Area created a jumble of impressions that left them bewildered and lost. No one was there to help them find a home or a job. No one was there to even smile or lend a hand. One day, after changing buses and walking miles all over Berkeley, Gosia, hot and exhausted, saw a sign on the back of a bench at a bus stop. It read "Welcome, Truman's Mortuary." She stared at it, aghast. This sign was for her a bleak welcome into a blemished, deathly land, and every bit of her fought to find optimism in this new life that she was thrust into.

She barely got along with her husband's cousin, who let them stay with her when they first arrived. For some reason, she never liked Gosia from the minute she laid eyes on her. She made it very clear that her job was done, priding herself on rescuing the family from their plight. With an evil eye and carefully placed sighs, she pointed at the door and bid the family farewell after two weeks. She had some friends who were leaving for Europe and arranged for her cousin and his family to stay in their apartment for a few months until Andrzej could find a job and they could afford their own place.

Agnieszka started junior high school and was miserable because she was so different from her classmates and her accent stood out, as did her braided hair and her unfashionable clothes.

* * *

A few days after they moved into the friend's apartment, Gosia walked the streets again, feeling lost. One day, she saw a tall, wooden, figure of a man in a blue uniform who was pointing to the left. She followed where it was pointing and entered a pretty wood building. There was soft music playing inside. She opened another door and came into a big hall with many benches. There was no one around. She was frightened and left quickly, noticing the sign on the front door that she hadn't noticed before. It was another mortuary.

What is this about, all this death, all this depression, all this morbidity in this bizarre country?

She came home that afternoon, ready to pack her suitcases, wanting to leave this place.

I want to move to Australia, a continent we have not yet been to.

She voiced her angst to her husband that night, her desire to leave.

"We can't leave now," he said in a quiet voice. "I have just been offered a good job at Bechtel."

Gosia looked at her husband, the glee in his eyes. She smiled back, trying to meet his joy. Underneath, she felt sadder than ever, knowing that now there could be no escape, no running away on her own accord. Her fate was now in the hands of this land that did not welcome her, that made her feel trapped, isolated and longing for home. Over the past several years she had been through so much. She was exhausted, overwhelmed and longed for something that had no words. She was grieving but did not even know it. She knew she should be grateful: she and her family were finally safe; her husband had a good job, and they were no longer being persecuted. But deep down, in the recesses of her brain was an unsettled grief that perhaps would never go away. From that knock on the door to the present, the world had changed, hatred had amassed to such ungainly proportions and much of her family had been slaughtered. She, her husband, and her two children, had barely survived the atrocities that lingered around them for all those years. What was left were skeletons of the heart, even if their bodies had pulled through. *Nothing would ever be the same*, she thought, over and over, as grief overcame her with a wave of nausea. She went to bed, telling her husband that she must have eaten something that was not right. She slept for twelve hours, after which she woke up and tried to start a new life.

Chapter Nineteen

Berkeley, California early spring 2024

I am downstairs, looking out at the San Francisco Bay, its many vacillating shades of blue, the San Bruno mountains in the distance and the Bay Bridge that spans the vast body of water. If I look closely, I can see tiny specks of cars and buses that make up the thousands that cross this bridge daily. Seventy years ago, my grandfather was one of those passengers, on the Key System train, going to and from San Francisco to his job at Bechtel.

I live in the garden apartment of the grand house that my grandparents bought in 1957, with the earnings my grandfather had made from his first stable employment in this country. When the realtor showed them this house in the hills at sunset in October, they fell in love with the beauty of the colors of the sky that reflected on the Bay, as if it was burning. Then the lights of San Francisco would appear like diamonds, continually mesmerizing them.

My aunt, Agnieszka, lived in this downstairs room while she attended Berkeley High School. She looked out the same window I am now peering out of. She listened to the birds call out from the lemon tree outside, the male to the female, welcoming spring and the end to the long winter of rains. It was here that my aunt took out her braids, lost her accent, and realized that in this country one did not care about where you are from, what trauma you have experienced. Denying the past and blending into the norm was the immigrant's task. When my aunt wasn't in the confines of her parents' rules, she was making friends, occasionally smoking and drinking and becoming popular. Her good looks and her intelligent, rebellious, ways led her on the path towards acceptance in this strange land that she began to devour. In her blossoming adolescence, she eagerly adopted the American *forget the past* attitude.

She couldn't have known then that the trauma and the grief from her formative years would reside inside her and lay dormant for decades, waiting for the right moment to burst through her body, creating for her in her older years a life filled with incessant pain that was never diagnosed, but was most probably fibromyalgia. Grief is that raw piece of glass, shattered. Its shards seep into the skin, the throat, the organs, the muscles, the blood stream, the fabric of a being, permanently scarring the heart for years and years after the wound has happened.

One month ago, she died.

I stare out the window watching birds. In her older years, she loved birds, their transcendence, their lightness in being and their fragility that in many ways matched hers. She was beautiful, brilliant, adventurous. She tried not to remember the pain, but in the end, it consumed her. I remember her laugh. Her smile. They lit up a room. She hated being old, hated that she was in pain all the time in her later years. In her quiet moments, she hated that she was never able to stop the poison that began to flow through her when she was two and was forced to leave her home while bombs exploded around her.

* * *

My mother never got to live in the grand house overlooking the bay. She lived with her parents in their first small apartment in downtown Berkeley until my father swept her off her feet and they got married and found a place of their own. Unlike her sister, my mother was not rebellious, adventurous, or a dreamer. She did not care if she was popular. Shortly after she arrived in Berkeley with a vomit-stained dress, my mother began her studies at the University of California Berkeley. About a year later, she was suddenly struck with tuberculosis and was sent to a sanatorium across the bay, where she had to isolate, breathe the cold air and undergo massive, invasive treatments that would end up scarring her lungs.

When she healed, and after she got married, she lived a life of caution, as prescribed by her doctor. When her first child was born, my oldest sister, she was not allowed to hold her for the first six months of her life, due to the belief at that time that she could still transmit the disease to her child. This theory was later refuted.

She later became a licensed psychotherapist, and for decades, listened to others' traumas, healing them. She was a fountain of love for her children and her clients, but never allowed herself to look within. She survived breast cancer when she was 70, heart disease and COPD. At 80, she fell and had to have a metal plate put into her hip, and then, after my dad passed in 2014, her brain began its long, progressive dementia.

Now, my 94-year-old mother is all that is left in my family of Holocaust survivors, my beautiful mother who hangs onto a sweet world of oblivion, where she smiles all the time, as long as no one brings up the word *death*, as long as no one reminds her of her childhood. The last time she spoke to her sister on the phone, a month before she died, she said over and over she loved her. Her sister said over and over she loved her. I wonder if they knew this would be the last time they would express these feelings. I wonder if her dementia paused for a moment to realize her sister was leaving her. There were so many years they had loved each other, without saying it. It wasn't until their older years that they could put words to their love. There was such a history that I, as her daughter, was not privy to. A few days after the death of her sister, my mother said her sister's name over and over, and then looked out the window. We asked her who is that person?

She replied, "She is my sister."

In the present tense.

* * *

I am in the woods, on the Olympic Peninsula in Washington State. My aunt's ashes have just been composted around old growth cedar trees. Then a moment of silence ensued as the stately trees, whose tops we cannot see, soaked in the nourishment we had just given them.

In a quiet, affirming voice the cantor chanted the Mourner's Kaddish:

Yitgadal v'yitkadash sh'mei raba b'alma di-v'ra
chirutei, v'yamlich malchutei b'chayeichon
uvyomeichon uvchayei d'chol beit yisrael, ba'agala
uvizman kariv, v'im'ru: "amen."
Y'hei sh'mei raba m'varach l'alam ul'almei almaya.
Yitbarach v'yishtabach, v'yitpa'ar v'yitromam
v'yitnaseh, v'yithadar v'yit'aleh v'yit'halal sh'mei
d'kud'sha, b'rich hu,
l'eila min-kol-birchata v'shirata, tushb'chata
v'nechemata da'amiran b'alma, v'im'ru: "amen."

Y'hei shlama raba min-sh'maya v'chayim aleinu
v'al-kol-yisrael, v'im'ru: "amen."
Oseh shalom bimromav, hu ya'aseh shalom aleinu
v'al kol-yisrael, v'imru: "amen."

* * *

The solar eclipse reached totality exactly the moment the cantor silently stood, the kaddish having been recited. We, breathless, all stared up at the tree, the endless tree, now enshrouded in complete darkness. In that awe-filled moment our grief surrounded us: grief for my aunt, grief for my ancestors, grief for all in my family who had perished in the Holocaust, grief for a suffering planet under the calloused hands of humanity who maims innocent souls.

Then the light began its return to the sky, and allowed us to breathe again, as we each picked up a stone, kissed it, and placed it at the base of the tree we were standing under, the oldest living tree in that forest.

Then we walked away in silence as the light followed us, and the sun re-emerged.

* * *

With my aunt gone, and my mother in her sweet place of innocence, it is my sisters, my cousins and I who now bear the infinitesimal loss of a family that survived such horrors, such displacement, such loss. My fragile petite body holds pain that I should not have been given, but alas, was. I came into this world, the fragile one, the one who cries, the one who holds the pen. It is impossible to bury grief when one is a pallbearer of emotions.

I am afraid of anger, quite truthfully, but if I stop and open the anger gates, I know I would wail.

I sense that grief *is* that wail I am so afraid of, that scream into the night with the windows open, the piercing howl, so forceful it peels off the protective layer of the lungs making me unable to speak, to eat, to live.

* * *

I stare at a tree outside my grandmother's house, a redwood that I planted after she passed away in 1991. It was six inches high then. It is huge now, its limbs tower into the sky. Those limbs are a home to all kinds of birds.

Some days this magnificent redwood tree does not move and stands still like a sentry. When there is a storm, however, and the rain and the wind jostle all the limbs, the tree shakes, and so many branches and seeds tumble to the earth. Some of the seeds fly to other parts of the neighborhood, but many stay within the domain of the grand tree, burying themselves deeply in the ground, continually perpetuating new growth.

Often, I feel like that tree, I resonate with its essence. I let myself sway with the wind; I create new life by writing.

I am called to remember, so many years earlier, what was on the other side of the fence. It all comes back to me as I look at the plethora of seeds strewn all over the ground. Weeds were everywhere that day, consuming every crevice of that space, ugly gangly plants, many of which had menacing thorns that looked like the haven of a monster yet, with a closer look, a truly closer look, I remember seeing the tiniest of shoots seemingly coming from nowhere... something green, something that looked like they wanted to grow and become beautiful.

I smile, and sigh, inhale and deeply exhale, feeling the peace of it all, knowing that I have worked so hard to find my truth, as I continue to gaze at that lone gorgeous tree surrounded by a cloud- filled sky.

Acknowledgements

I have waited thirty -three years for this moment.

Sitting in my grandmother's dining room that looks out to the San Francisco Bay, feeling my Baba's presence, remembering her perfume, her thick accent, the smells of baking in the kitchen, I am taken back to the time when I was young and there was only sweetness.

Since her passing in 1991, we have had consistent tenants occupying this home.

Finally, three weeks ago, the last of the tenants moved out, and for the first time since the 4th of November 1991, the day my grandmother left us, I am alone in this grand house, feeling comforted by the history, the memories, the whisper of her spirit that resides in these walls.

I have gone through a long, often painful journey to understand, to put the pieces together, to forge that path away from the innocence of my childhood to where I am now. This home represented healing, healing from the scars of Europe, from the wails of the ancestors who perished, from all the trauma that occurred in the lives of my beloved family.

In this grand dining room, in this house, finally again in this house, I feel the hope that my grandparents must have felt that day in October when the realtor showed them this place in the Berkeley Hills, at sunset, and the skies were swirling with orange.

Thank you to this home, that brings it all together, that housed the happy times, the love in my family, that created a pulsing energy that inspired my grandparents to move on and thrive.

Thank you to my Dziadzia, my late grandfather, for being that rock, for holding the world on your shoulders, for bringing the family to safety time after time. And thank you for recording your version of the family story, in Polish, that my mother and my aunt translated into English.

Thank you to my Baba, my late grandmother, for inspiring us all to think, to know, to understand. Thank you for softening your harder edges so that we could remember you as the nurturer you became once this home enveloped your soul. And thank you for writing down your version of the family story in the Holocaust autobiography group you were part of at the Jewish Community Center in Berkeley.

Thank you to my late aunt Zosia for always being an inspiration to me, one who defies the banal, who does not take no for an answer, and, like her parents, uses the intellect to survive.

Thank you to my late father for being that shining horse, that gentle, caring man for my mother and for the whole family, even if you were a non-Jewish American and had no idea what your wife had been through.

Thank you to my mother, my precious 94-year-old demented mother whom I love and cherish with a limitlessness, who no longer has a memory of her blighted past, and whose sweetness has only grown and grown and grown.

Thank you to my two older sisters whom I have adored since I was little. I know I was sometimes a pest to you, growing up. It was all part of the googy state I found myself in, surrounded by all those unanswered questions I finally understand now, so many years later.

Thank you to Aude Ramadier, my angel, my editor, who understands and believes in me and my need to tell this story, who knows how to make my writing as good as it can be.

Thank you to my sister Vicki, the English professor, who followed in my grandmother's footsteps, and has brilliantly mastered the art of language. Thank you for reading this manuscript so carefully and for providing me with your invaluable critique, and your astute knowledge of our family history.

And thank you to Sharon Blyth-Moss for your stunning book cover design that describes so eloquently not only what I saw that day, peering over the fence, but also what I saw inside me, my own family history, that emerged over time.

And finally, thank you, as always, to Kathy Campbell and the entire crew at Gorham Printing, for your continual excellence in the design and production of this, and all my books.

About the Author

Heidi Harrison, author of *The Four Seasons* (Sapphire Books Publishing), and *When Paris Was Her Lover* (Emerald House Publishing) has always loved writing. At a very early age, she realized that words allowed for the exodus of her soul, a rhapsody, a sense of grace enveloping her. Writing has been her boulder, her stories the healing balm in a world that sometimes cries out for this. She was born and raised in the San Francisco Bay Area. She holds a MS degree in Counseling Psychology, and a dual degree in Child Development and French, and she spent almost thirty years as a psychotherapist and a teacher of young children. She is also a classically trained violinist. She has traveled extensively between the hemispheres and has lived and studied in Paris and in Grenoble, France. She has written several novels and children's books, countless stories, (fiction and creative nonfiction) and a full-length memoir. In each of these works, she is inspired by imagination itself, by real stories of people's lives, by love, by music, by the stunning majesty of nature, by the beauty and power of words, relationships, the diversity of cultures, and the resiliency of the human heart. We live in a complicated and often challenging world, and yet, as a writer, an observer, and as a teacher, she is, every day, inspired by the grace and by the infinite beauty that we, as humans, embody. Our dazzling earth is of an infinite nature; humbly, she lets words only begin to describe it.

Website: www.heidimharrison.com

Facebook: https://www.facebook.com/HeidiEmeraldHarrison.Author/